Absolute
Bull

A Cable Counties Thriller

Hartley Stevens

In all respects, this novel is a work of fiction.

Names, places, and incidents are either the product of the author's imagination or are used fictitiously. Any resemblance to actual persons, living or dead, or to actual events or locales is unintentional and coincidental.

ISBN: 978-1-944941-01-7 (ebook)
ISBN: 978-1-944941-02-4 (print)

Published in the United States of America
By, Big Toe Writes, LLC.

Cover design by Derek Murphy
www.creativindiebookcovers.com

Editing, formatting and layout provided by
Polgarus Studio
www.polgarusstudio.com

Website Design by Sharon Julien
www.sjulien.com

Original songs by Douglas Haines
www.douglashainesmusic.com

For Jeanie
Love & Life

Contents

Absolute Bull

Absolute: (ab-so-loot); *adj.* not qualified or diminished in any way; total.
Synonyms: complete, total, utter, out-and-out, outright, entire, perfect, pure, decided.

Bull: (bool); *n.* an uncastrated male bovine animal. *adj.* of a part of the body corresponding to the part of a male bovine animal in build and strength. *v.* push or drive powerfully or violently.
Synonyms: ample, bulky, capacious, considerable, prodigious, idiocy, insanity, unreasonableness.

Prologue

The Running of the Bulls, Pamplona, Spain, 1999

Fredrico Bataan and Tessa, his tart for the weekend, pressed their faces against the train's steamed windows as it came to a final stop. The mood in the passenger car grew to a frenzy by the time the wheels screeched to a halt. The train was filled with young people from around the world, most of them American. The air was charged with testosterone and the entitled youth made their presence known with boastful chants.

Fredrico hated the Americans. He was the son of a wealthy landowner from Madrid and an American mother. She loved Europe, not for its historical glory, but for its traditions and pretensions to culture.

It wasn't his custom to travel with the common dregs of society. Only several bottles of sangria the night before and the promise of Tessa opening the petals of her most desired flower convinced him to travel to Pamplona.

They took the overnight train from Barcelona to participate in the San Fermin Festival—the Running of the Bulls. He'd come to the festival many times as a child and later as an eager young adult. For Fredrico, there was no more sex-starved, adrenaline induced gathering in the entire world, save maybe the Brazilian Rio Carnival.

Fredrico's head still swam with sangria. He hadn't yet dipped into the pain of a hangover.

He and Tessa stumbled from the train, bags in hand. Several travelers lay in their own vomit around the floor of the train station. He kicked his way through, rather than shuffle. He couldn't believe he'd allowed any woman, even the beautiful Tessa, to convince him to come here. Pamplona was *passé*; there were so many parties of much more substance and opportunity.

The first of many dirty maidens approached him with attire items for the run. At Tessa's urging he finally let one place a fire-red hat resembling a flattened mushroom with an erection on his head. Another looped a red kerchief around his neck. He paid them both.

He drew the line at riding with this unruly mob on a city bus. He searched for a taxi and finally hailed one down. It was a twenty-minute ride into the heart of the ancient city. There was no rain, but the windshield wipers, adorned with red lacing, beat a furious pace back and forth. The driver thought himself expert—Fredrico thought him a fool.

Fredrico tried to calm his mind on the ride. Drunken sex was the best kind in his estimation. It got rid of any inhibitions and let lovers act out the animal lust buried beneath a shroud of decency. Tonight he would experiment—he would push the envelope and use the new tool he'd conceived from his dark imagination. Tessa was the right kind. Of course, she would be willing to do the normal stuff. But she also wouldn't hesitate to let him find new horizons of ecstasy when they were deep in the gulf of alcoholic passion.

Fredrico was a man accustomed to the finer things. He didn't earn these things, but instead inherited the life of a prince. He couldn't find satisfaction in work of any kind. Normal production was beneath him. In his estimation, there were simply different classes of people. Some were put here on earth to till the soil or work in the factories, and some were meant to *own* the soil and factories. Certain rewards were Fredrico's because of his station and his intellect. He believed, like Stalin, that power came from the barrel of a gun. People were motivated by violence. This applied equally to workers in the factory, the field, and in the bedroom.

If sex didn't hurt, then you probably weren't doing it right.

The taxi jerked to a stop in the heart of the ancient city and they got out. Standing in the Plaza Castillo, Fredrico gaped at the revelry and mayhem on all sides. A loud speaker bellowed, "*Viva San Fermin*" as the mayor proclaimed the beginning of the day's festivities.

Fredrico was calculating his sexual plans for the evening when around him erupted a chorus of "*Toro. Toro. Toro.*" This was a call from the novice as well as the experienced runners. A small group of locals were moving toward the narrow opening of the plaza. Fredrico followed.

Tessa positioned herself near the entrance of the coliseum. There, she would be able to take snap-shots of her man as he bravely ran in front of the devilish herd.

The crowd of runners was picking up its pace. A cannon's deafening roar broke the morning, and the white and red-clad revelers began to trot. Fredrico did the same.

Fredrico had never run with the bulls even though he'd come to Pamplona many times. Pushed by the alcohol in his system and the need to appear brave in Tessa's eyes, he found himself in the madness of the throng.

Suddenly it didn't seem like such a good idea.

In the distance behind him he heard the first soft scrape of hooves. His pulse quickened as many of the runners began to sprint, and Fredrico did the same. Now the blood hammered his skull.

Ten seconds later, the hooves were slapping the stones with anger. He looked over his shoulder for the first time and saw the beasts, the bulls, six abreast and tearing through the narrow street. Fear filled him, and the need to *run* was the only thing on his mind.

Ahead, a hairpin turn was plugged with bodies squirming to free themselves. Fredrico didn't feel like one of the rank and file. He was *special*— a bullet that would slam into the mass of bodies and by sheer force and will-power reach safety on the other side. He threw himself headfirst into the horde. It didn't give.

Instead, it actually repelled him.

Looking over his shoulder again, he saw the bulls frothing at the mouth, scared and angry at the human spectacle. At the turn, emergency crews leaned over the wooden fences and screamed frantically for the runners to break the bottleneck.

Behind him, an elderly man pleaded with true fear in his eyes for the runners in front to hurry. Fredrico was at the center of the mass and saw the high board fence as his only salvation. He lunged toward it and looked back at the closing hooves at the same time. His divided gaze meant Fredrico fell short and he landed on the panicked crowd.

The terrified bulls never broke stride. They hit the mob of humanity six abreast with horns, slobber, and hate. The old Spaniard crumpled beneath the hooves, then Fredrico felt the sharp point of a bull's horn impale him below the waist. With tremendous strength, the bull shook his head and threw Fredrico against the hard stone wall, kicking him repeatedly in the head as he collapsed to the cobblestone street.

Bodies were all around him. Wails of pain and fear filled the formerly festive air. Fredrico felt no pain, but he reached a trembling hand toward his middle.

He looked to his right and saw a blood-smeared lump of flesh splayed out like a contortionist's dream. *What was that?* His consciousness told him this might be something important, but what? *Who am I… why am I here?* He couldn't raise the memory. He sat beside the grotesque lump with one hand resting near his bleeding crotch. He bellowed a deep heinous sound which pierced the noise of the maddening crowd.

As he sat laughing his sanity away, a pair of men in white coveralls came to his side. The men were dark silhouettes, even in the morning sun. They spoke to each other in a sharp, impenetrable dialect.

Fredrico continued his lunatic cackle as the men bent over the lump of something he should remember. After pressing his head to the breast of the lump, one of the men shouted in some commotion of words Fredrico could no longer hear.

A small, harried man emerged from the crowd and stood looking down at the maniacally laughing form of Fredrico Bataan. A wicked smile crossed the man's lips as he took a metallic syringe from his white coat and brandished it in front of Fredrico's wet wild eyes, before jabbing the needle into Fredrico's throat.

Fredrico's mind sailed away into a hallucination of a menacing black knight straddling a scaled serpent, riding the writhing neck as he slammed a sword deep into the head of the beast.

That day, that very minute, on the cobblestone streets of Pamplona, Fredrico Bataan ceased to exist. On the ashes of his still-living corpse, the men from the Institute began building their future international terrorist, Bent Daleen.

Chapter 1

The Cable Counties, Florida

Except for light from the lunar peach moon, the night was dark, filled with a hundred million mosquitoes and the sound of cicadas.

The dozen or so dark figures danced and whooped. The lust of Sodom and Gomorrah filled their hearts and they gave themselves utterly to the moment.

Long and tall, a singular figure emerged, clad in olive drab camouflage with an ancient rendition of a lightning bolt caressing a purple oval painted on his naked chest. He held his hands high and called out to the dancers.

"Seekers, children of a greater god, see the emblem of the masses at its worst. I am the Prophet, Bent Daleen."

With that, the man showed them a glass jar with two severed human ears floating in a clear liquid. He placed it reverently next to the body of the slaughtered bull.

"Hell truly hath no fury like the Prophet who has lost his faith in mankind."

Chapter 2

My name is Jeremiah St. Cloud.

From time to time I solve problems. Recently I'd been called a private detective and worse. All of the monikers were probably accurate and were earned—the hard way.

It was Thursday. I was sitting at the Lawless Diner finishing the last pages of *Catcher in The Rye*. This was the fifth time I'd read the book and I still didn't understand what the hell Holden Caulfield was all about. Salinger was a nemesis of sorts, and I wouldn't quit until I could understand the genius. Shrimp and grits were on the way, so I was working hard not to drool. That's when old Ben McCullers staggered into the restaurant, three sheets to yonder wind.

His sun-worn face was slick with perspiration and tears were raining down between the cracks. Before I could get there, he knocked a bowl of mints off the pay counter and cussed two guys he'd known all his life. One of the men cursed Ben back, and I gave him a look which made him sit back down to his grits and gravy.

Making rough snorting sounds, Ben slumped against the counter. I grabbed him by the shoulders and he let me guide him over to my table. Plopping down, he accepted a cloth napkin from Molly, the owner, and wiped at his face like a three-year-old. He honked hard into the napkin and handed it back to Molly. He peered across the table, and I saw the drunken haze lift enough so he recognized me.

"Cloud." It came out in two syllables Cli-yowd. "I'm-a been looking for ya." He slurred all the words into one somewhat coherent line. "Basssards… basssards kilt my Billy."

I motioned to Molly and set a twenty on the table. With some effort we pushed and begged Ben out the back door and into my truck.

***

He mumbled some and blubbered plenty as I drove towards Sandspur, his five-hundred-acre ranch. An immaculate white board fence announced the entrance, and I drove down the lane to his house. The grass leading up to the lane was a brighter green than the fields on either side. A hundred or so Black Angus cows dotted the fields, looking up unconcerned as we drove past. Dozens of buzzards rode the heat just beyond the rise to the north.

By the time we arrived at his home, Ben was passed out with his face smeared against the window of the truck. It was hot, summertime in central Florida, and no way could I let him sleep it off in the truck. He didn't cooperate as I evicted him from the cab and he swung on me twice, before I could get him in the house and into an abused and tattered recliner. Ben was seventy years old or so and drunk. The punches didn't do much even when they connected.

There was no air conditioning. I don't know why I was surprised. Ben put every cent he ever made back into Sandspur. I found an oscillating fan in a hall closet and turned it on. It felt like it might be a while, so I went out onto his porch and found a bench swing.

***

The nap on the swing didn't seem very long, but when I woke up and checked my watch, it was nearly two hours later. Ben was sitting in a rocker across from me looking a little soberer, but still deep in sorrow.

He saw I was awake. "They killed Billy." He pointed with his eyes to the circling vultures just over the rise.

I sat up and rubbed at the stubble on my face. "Who Ben? Who's Billy, and who killed him?"

8

He shook his head and rolled his eyes. "Billy… you know Billy. He's my bull—was anyhow. He was the boss, boy. One of a kind champion sire. Now, he's dead. Sorry sack-a-shit hunters."

"I'm sorry to hear that. He must've been special."

"I need you to find 'em. Find 'em and kill 'em."

Ben had played a role in my upbringing. He wasn't a central character, but he was always there. In the years I'd known him, I'd never seen him so distressed.

"Ben, c'mon now. Just settle down. Tell me what happened. We'll sort things out."

He shook his head violently. "Don't want to do no sortin'. I want you to find 'em and kill 'em."

He was making some assumptions about my past life based on gossip.

"Ben, you do know I don't do that? Kill people, I mean?" I was looking him straight in the eyes when I said it. His eyes said he was thinking about lying to me, playing the dumb card, the sympathy for the old coot card.

His face broke a little. It wasn't exactly a smile, but it was treacherous. "Yeah, but ya did. Back then. Didn't ya?"

I continued to look at him, noncommittal.

He rubbed at his whiskers. "Kill 'em Cloud. Just whip their asses and kill 'em in a bad way."

I nodded. "Listen, you need—"

"What I hear is… you fix problems." Ben was a hard man, made so by time, farming, weather, and the loss of a wife and a son.

I thought about asking where he'd heard that, but I really didn't want to know. "I'll do it for you, Ben. No killing, but I'll help. Whatever you heard, don't go passing on the gossip. I'm doing a favor for you, a friend."

It was his turn to nod.

I said, "You mentioned hunters before. You got anybody in mind?"

He shook his head. "Country boys been sneaking onto Sandspur for thirty years to hunt and fish. I run 'em off, they come back. For the most part they're just living the country-boy way. But I can't imagine any of 'em killin' Billy."

"Who've you run off lately?"

"Nobody."

"Nobody?"

He said, "Nobody I know. Nobody I know could've done this. They burned him. Cut his tail and ears off and burned him down to bone. Couldn't be anybody I know, right?"

I got up to leave and said, "I reckon I'll go ask *them*."

Chapter 3

It was hard seeing that rock of a man I'd known most of my life in so much pain. He was heartsick and hurting in the worst possible way. That bull was a pet, but more like family since he didn't have family anymore.

Heading down state road 100, the truck just kind of turned itself into the entrance of a prairie-born cattle field. The cows in this field weren't nearly as handsome as the ones back at Sandspur. They were hugely fat and marked of every color. They were curs, mutts, what we country folk call free-range bovine bitches. I'll give 'em this, they all—I mean every one—had a mini duplicate, a calf tugging at swollen nipples.

Over the range and through the woods to MacGregor Knox's house I went. Driving through the pines and over-hanging oaks it looked more like the secret entrance to the Bat Cave than the winding drive to a country farm house.

It was a Cracker house—old Florida. But the house wasn't old. Knox built it just four or five years ago when he retired from the NFL. The yard was a garden, every manner of native Florida plant growing at full move.

In attendance, besides the native plants, was a healthy woman, seven peacocks I could count, a young blood hound, and one long, tall country boy eating a tomato like an apple. Knox tossed what was left of the tomato over the fence and walked over with a big red smile. He was shirtless and the red juice leaked down his front over a carved and hairless chest.

The lady of the garden waved, and I waved back. I said, "Isn't that Mrs.

Toomey Martin?"

He nodded.

"She doesn't look as if she's here on a landscaping assignment."

Another nod.

"Broken heart, broken house?"

A shrug this time.

"Toomey will be pissed when she goes back to him."

"Yeah, there'll be that."

He didn't want to talk about his philandering. I changed the subject. "When you gonna get a truck and stop driving around in that suped-up El Camino?"

"It's a truck, anus. Notice the wide tires, four-wheel drive I might add, the bed of pure pewter and gun metal gray."

I rolled my eyes. "Says Che-vro-let on the tailgate. That means car my friend. Chevy builds a hell of car, wins two outta three NASCAR races."

"It's a truck."

"Dodge Ram, that's a truck. Ford sometimes. Chevy and all the rest, ain't nothin' but cars."

"Fuck you," he said.

"Right back at you, big daddy."

***

After a few more minutes insulting each other for sport, Knox and I walked up the railroad tie steps and into the air-conditioned loveliness of his home. He returned from the refrigerator with two cold beers, and I followed him into the game room. He called it the game room, but really your choices were pool or darts. If one's tastes ran to the modern electronic variety, then one would be sorely disappointed.

Knox racked the balls. He drained half the beer and wiped his mouth with the back of his arm.

"How're you doing Mr. Agent-In-Charge?" I said

"You know I've been suspended for going on a month now. I reckon you can stop calling me that."

"Never. I still enjoy the irony. You being a law enforcer and all."

He used a smooth stroke and broke the balls. They exploded from the triangle. A yellow one teetered on the edge of the corner pocket, then gave way to gravity and disappeared down the hole.

He lined up another shot. "Ben McCullers' bull got killed last night." I said.

"Yeah, I heard." He sank another ball.

Of course I knew he'd heard. He might be removed from the Cable Department of Law Enforcement, involuntarily, but he always knew what was happening in his counties.

"Tell me about it."

"I think it's reaching epidemic proportions."

"How so?"

"Because including Billy last night, there've been three in all. They're spread out over the Cable Counties—one in Levy County, one in Marion County, and now Billy here in Alachua County."

"Anything unusual about the scenes?"

"Scenes no, not really, the bulls yeah. They all had their ears and tails cut off. Then they were burned like some kind of sacrifice."

I knew serial killers sometimes took a souvenir, a little trophy. I'd heard of the same behavior directed towards animals. "Why you reckon that is?"

"Sicko trophy hunters are my guess. Some of these good ole boys just have to be killing something all the time. When deer or turkeys or anything else isn't in season, they still need to hunt. The burning, I have no idea."

I moved the white ball away from in front of his cue. He looked up annoyed. "Bullshit!" I said. "We've known each other since the Academy and one thing I know for sure is you always have an idea. And, I tell ya, I get the feeling you're holding back on your best friend. Tell me."

He threw his cue stick on the table in disgust—an uncharacteristic surge of emotion. "What people don't know is that before the first bull was found a year or so ago, there was a body. A human body. A female we've still not identified because she was burned so bad we can't even get good dentals. And you know what else?"

I was cold somber now. No joking around. I shook my head.

"She was missin' her ears and teeth."

"You'd a thought that would've made the papers."

He picked up the cue and put it back in the rack. "Yeah, you would."

***

MacGregor Knox has been my best friend since our Academy days at West Point. Our trails diverged after he took an early-out following our stint in the Desert Wars. The Army let him go and the Cowboys immediately swooped him up in the NFL draft. He spent eleven years in their employ. During that time, I stayed on with the military in more shadowy jobs.

Cable County isn't an actual county. It's a tightly woven belt of thirteen central Florida counties that for more than a hundred years have pooled their resources to differentiate themselves from Florida's pan-handle Yankee tourist and the millions of import liberal sinners to the south. The actual names of the counties are Levy, Alachua, Clay, Bradford, Marion, Gilchrist, St. John's, Flagler, Dixie Columbia, Volusia, Union, and Putnam. Each county has its own law enforcement, but there exists an overarching authority referred to as the Cable Department of Law Enforcement. MacGregor Knox was the he-coon, tippy-top Agent-In-Charge of all of Cable. He reported directly to the Governor of Florida and absolutely no one else.

For different reasons, we both saw our time come to an end with our respective employers. Being a Cable native, I moved back. Knox moved to Cable because he didn't really have anywhere else calling him. We both enjoyed living close to each other in the central Florida belt called the Cable Counties.

Chapter 4

Bent Daleen in Florida, the Scrub

The plan was coalescing nicely. Nobody could predict the reckoning to come.

It had taken some time pulling together this chapter of the Seekers congregation, three years in all. Three years to incubate the poison.

Bent Daleen lived deep in the innards of the huge swamp the locals called the Scrub. The compound was spare, built within the remainders of a World War II supply depot.

The loyal followers numbered just a hundred or so. Some were imports from successful terrorist campaigns throughout the world. A few were local recruits, disgruntled farm and ranch hands, who needed something to belong to. The Seekers organization was as good as any other for those boys.

On the table in front of him he admired two dozen clear jars. The jars were filled with formaldehyde. In each one, suspended within the preservative, floated two human ears.

***

1999 – The Institute, Barcelona, Spain

The Institute had been in existence far longer than anyone could prove or disprove. Deep in the recesses of a cavernous vault inside an ancient building off Rambles—a pedestrian highway in Barcelona—the successful ventures of the Institute were chronicled.

On one well-preserved wall was the painting of a battle. Below it was a worn sheaf of paper describing the fight between the young warrior Alexander and Darius. On another wall was a primitive rendition of a young shepherd named David, wheeling a slingshot over his head towards a giant Philistine named Goliath.

The Crusades, The Boer Wars, the fall of the Greek and Roman Empires, the assassination of Arch Duke Ferdinand, and even a detailed painting of three men hanging on crosses on a lone hill were masterfully displayed on the walls.

More recent pictorials included a spectral flag in the shape of a broken cross and a bright white flag with a single red dot being hoisted above a sinking aircraft carrier. Another portrayed an entire city being engulfed by flames on one of Ireland's coastal cities.

Within one of several filing cabinets were black and white photographs. Among these were pictured a skinny brown youth running naked, her flesh boiling with Napalm. Another showed the Third Reich passing through the *Arc de Triomphe*. And yet another portrayed a threesome of black hanging bodies against the steam of a Louisiana swamp.

There was a clay model of the moment when Martin Luther King was shot. Another likeness, again in clay, was of an open convertible in Dallas.

In the vault were weapons, too. Long past their prime, these trophies served as a remembrance of days past. Signatures of the absolute lords of terror throughout the ages were scrawled on their outer casings.

On the ceiling was an elaborate painting of Cain slaying Able.

***

Over several years, the men at the Institute manufactured the character and life of whoever would become Bent Daleen. These same men roughly sketched the future their new creation would follow. They had very high expectations for their latest soldier.

When the dossier was complete, they waited for the right opportunity and exactly the right man to host their blueprint for terror. Fredrico Bataan was just such a man.

Bataan, now Daleen, had led as close to a stress-free life as seemed possible. Growing up wealthy, he didn't fret over the usual hardships life threw at everyday people. Because of this, his mind was remarkably unscarred. Privileged as he was, Bataan had been a vain man. He kept his body in top physical condition in order to woo the affections of women.

Bataan had now been within the confines of the Institute for nineteen months. His recovery had been slow, but that was due to the alterations the Institute doctors made rather than his injuries. Bataan suffered near complete amnesia, a condition his saviors and now captors found extremely suitable to their needs. The accident with the bulls also left Bataan unable to procreate, but this was also of benefit. The men from the Institute felt an *undistracted* soldier was a more focused killing machine.

The crucial alterations made to Fredrico were inside his brain. The Institute had an interest, a mission to continue the evolution of man. Their premise was that mankind certainly needed to struggle against nature, but it also needed to struggle against his fellow man.

A case study of two tribes of Neanderthals served as their primary evidence. Archeologists and anthropologists discovered two tribes that existed in what was now modern day France. At this time, the planet was almost entirely unpopulated by Homo sapiens. They could have gone anywhere and claimed any and all land as their own. Instead, the two tribes fought each other bitterly for hundreds of years. The man-against-man conflict produced within each culture more educated generations with the ability to form tools, develop a language, and even have a rudimentary form of commerce.

Man needed to have an enemy, a *human* enemy, in order to evolve. The mission of the Institute was to create men who could incite struggle and conflict within the masses. Bent Daleen would be such a man.

They re-engineered him by deep suggestion and hypnosis to believe a very different history of himself. Fredrico Bataan the former playboy, rich kid ne'er-do-well was now Bent Daleen, an Institution terrorist. They gave him memories of commanding mercenaries carrying out the most ghoulish missions. He was given motor-memory supporting a vast knowledge and acumen in the martial arts. They engineered him to believe the government— all governments—were oppressive and constructed to calm the great masses into a sense of satisfaction with less. In the deepest recesses of his new mind, Bent Daleen was a fierce, cold-blooded killer who loved his work and wouldn't hesitate to take risks with his own life and the people he commanded.

Fully healed, Bent Daleen moved to a secret military training compound. The next year of his life was spent honing the skills inserted into his brain. He received additional training on how to recruit people to help him carry out future missions. He was given no specific agenda, but his mind was washed into a state of high anxiety toward governmental control of the individual. Daleen was trained to be an army of one—trained alone to do work that would be lonely. He'd never need the social rewards of a job well done.

Following those first nineteen months, two other trainees joined Daleen. One of the men looked exactly like him. The trainers from the Institute referred to the three of them by numbers instead of names, but Daleen learned that one man was called Tito Salazar. His look-alike's name was Luis Alvarez.

They spent the next year of their lives in a mock POW camp in Cambodia. Here the men's bodies were developed to the point they could keep up with their re-engineered minds. They were schooled in the use of explosives, weaponry, hand-to-hand combat and mind control on prisoners.

On the final day of their training a member of the Institute brought the three men into a small shack. When everyone was seated he told them, "Gentlemen, the Mayan civilization brought about its own downfall. They suffered a condition the masses all seem to crave, *indifference.* There is a greater chance of man's dominance on this planet coming to an end through world peace rather than through the greatest of wars."

Assured the men were hanging on his every word, he went on, "It's not God's way to seek less struggle. He himself provides all manner of natural calamity such as pestilence, famine, and plague. We, the Seekers of Truth, will carry on the evolution of man. When man fights against man, it lets him assign blame, weed out the weak and stay as far away from apathy as possible.

Fear motivates man more than any benevolent undertaking."

Project "Bent Daleen" was among the most successful cases the men from the Institute had ever trained. The three men were pronounced masters in every facet of their reengineering.

With that, the three men were turned loose on the world.

Chapter 5

The Cable Counties, Florida

Mid-afternoon brought the kind of sticky heat only central Florida seems able to produce. I'd arranged a meeting with Tom Goodrich, the president of the local cattlemen's association. He didn't seem interested in speaking with me at first, but I can be very persuasive. He said he'd meet me in town for lunch. I suggested the Lawless Diner, and he agreed.

So I found myself at midday, sitting at the same table where this case started for me that morning with Ben. Molly Lawless' restaurant is a country kitchen. It serves exactly the kind of food you would imagine, whether you're country or not. Each day there is a *special*. Monday's is meatloaf with mashed potatoes and gravy, Tuesday is chicken and dumplings, Wednesday fried chicken, and so on. Today was Thursday and that meant country-fried steak, a personal favorite. The Lawless serves home style. There are no menus. You get the special of the day or you just have iced tea—sweet iced tea. Molly and her husband Frank own the place and know every single person in town.

Molly came right over. "What ya say, Heaven-Above-Number-One?"

"Never trust a skinny cook," I said.

"Well then, I must be the most untrustworthy person in the Cable Counties."

"Fella by the name of Tom Goodrich is coming in to talk to me. Do you know him?"

"Yeah, I know Tom. Big rancher, president of the local Cattlemen's Association. He's from up north, one of them states starts with "I." I don't hold that against him though like some people would."

"He your kind of people?"

"He's a flirt, always talking about cowboy crap. He's mighty proud of the fact he's the president of that *association*. Always talking about that, too."

"I'll just have some sweet tea until he gets here."

"I'll bring it right out, sugar."

On Fridays during football season Molly always feeds the local high school team a meal before the game. Once, when I was a junior in high school, I had a rather bad motorcycle accident early in the summer. I was in the hospital for three weeks. Molly snuck my favorite meal into the hospital each Friday. Along with the help of Doc McCoy, they fixed me right up and I didn't miss a game.

The sweet iced tea came in a glass the size of a flowerpot. I did no sipping but guzzled it half gone. Tom Goodrich walked up to the table just as I was in the "Ahhh" part of finishing my long gulp.

"Mr. St. Cloud, I'm Tom Goodrich," he said, extending his hand. I shook it instead of wiping my mouth with the sleeve of my shirt.

Molly brought two plates piled high and just about to overflow. She set them in front of us and grabbed a wicker basket full of biscuits too. She looked at me and a twinkle graced her eyes. She didn't have to say anything; she knew she had set us up real fine.

Tom seemed to understand. We were going to eat first, then we would talk about the case. I grabbed a bottle of Tabasco sauce and shook it generously over everything on my plate. I offered Tom the bottle, but he only shook his head, a little disgusted with what I'd done.

I would love it if food lasted longer, but when in the presence of good country cooking, I'm a bit of a pig. I was finished before the rancher was halfway through.

Tom felt he should begin the conversation at this point. I held up my hand and told him to enjoy his meal, then we'd get to business. I pulled a scrap of the *New York Times* from my pocket and finished the crossword puzzle while he worked on his country-fried steak.

Tom finished his food and piled his fork, knife, and napkin on the spent plate. Before he could begin the conversation, a slim boy with a limp cleared the table and wiped the checkered tablecloth.

"Mr. St. Cloud, you said on the phone this had something to do with the bulls being killed around here."

"It's Cloud. Just Cloud—no mister—no saint."

"All right—the bulls?"

"Yes, what do you know about them?"

He raised his eyebrows. "And why would you be needing to know?"

Ah, give and take. My least favorite part of fixing problems. "Tom—may I call you Tom? A long-time friend of mine has been the victim of one of those killings, and he's asked for my assistance."

From his expression, Tom didn't feel we should be on a first name basis quite yet. "May I ask who that friend might be?" he asked.

"Yes."

Tom waited a second. So did I. I can play the give and take game as well as anyone.

"Well, who is it?"

"Ben McCullers."

He leaned back in his chair, relaxed or respectful, I wasn't sure which. "Ben is a long-standing member of the association, a very special and esteemed member." He was implying he couldn't imagine why in the world old, *respected* Ben would associate with a bug such as myself.

I helped him along. "So, in light of Ben's honored status within the organization, what the hell do you know about the bull killings?"

"There's no need to get rude."

I raised my eyebrows, mimicking him, and said nothing.

"So, Ben has hired you to find the killer?"

I nodded. This was fun.

"I should tell you, I'm interviewing skilled investigators. I hope to have a good man on the case within the week."

I was growing weary of the back and forth. Maybe if I took Tom out back and slapped him around some I would feel better.

"Tom, are you trying to tell me in your own convoluted way, you don't know a damned thing?" He was searching for the appropriate response, but I couldn't wait. "Give me the name of someone you might direct your *skilled investigator* towards when you finally hire him."

The search for a response to put me in my place was done, and the best Goodrich could muster was, "Ben may have hired you, but I don't care for you one bit."

"I'm used to that. Give me a name."

He was very red in the face by now. He might have been thinking about taking *me* out back from his body language. "What I'm telling you is on Ben's account."

"Okay."

"The Gallagher boys."

"Why them?"

Tom had brought a manila folder with him, making sure it was out of my reach when he put it down. Now he pushed it across the table towards me. "Because I don't know anybody else to look into right now."

I grabbed the file, threw a twenty on the table, and nodded at Tom. He looked away.

Chapter 6

There was still some light left in the sky, so I decided to go ahead and have a talk with the Gallagher boys.

Riding up the limestone road to the broken down house trailer the Gallagher's called home, I reminded myself not to stereotype people. Just because these boys were redneck white trash didn't necessarily mean they were the killers of prized bulls.

Pulling into their yard I saw a scene reminiscent of a Jeff Foxworthy joke. *If you have one big four-wheel drive in front of your house and three old cars sitting up on cement blocks, you might be a redneck.*

The truck was covered in gray black mud and had two long CB antennas bolted on either side of the rear bumper. A gun rack in the back window held a scoped rifle and a twelve-gauge shotgun. You could just make out the guns through the shade of a rebel flag draped across the rear window. As I pulled into the yard, two old bloodhounds dashed from under the trailer. A pit bull and some cur of unknown origin followed. All four dogs surrounded the door of my truck and were yelping and growling as if to say to each other, "dinner time."

I reached behind the seat and grabbed a hickory branch I keep for just such occasions. As soon as I opened the door and got both feet on the ground, the pit bull lunged at me with lust in his eyes and intent jaws. I looked hard at the pit, and with a feathered yet strong voice I said, "No." I brushed a worn denim leg against his barred teeth as I walked casually forward. The dog seemed stunned. He stopped, scratched one paw over greasy eye boogers, turned, and ran back under the trailer. The rest of the flea-ridden pack trailed him. Obviously he was the Alpha Male.

Amos Gallagher stood on the steps of his palace. He was wearing denim overalls and a dingy wife-beater T-shirt. The straps of his overalls were dangling, and he was the picture of redneck lore. He limped down the steps and crossed the muddy swamp of a yard over to where I stood with hickory in hand.

"What the fuck you want, Cloud?"

"Just wanted to shoot the bull, or rather, ask you some questions about shooting bulls," I said.

"Why the fuck you hit my dog? Some people get mighty riled when uninvited motherfuckers drive up and just start whaling on their dogs."

"Didn't have to hit. *Petunia* there doesn't seem to have much in the way of manners. I thought you might appreciate me helping you teach her a few."

"Dog's name ain't Petunia. That there is Spade, and I don't want nobody teaching that dog nothing 'ceptin me."

"Spade," I smiled. "What a colorful name. You come up with that?"

"Yeah, I named him. And color was just what I was thinking 'bout when I did."

"Dog's a bit of a sissy, ya ask me, Amos. I barely even nudged him and he whined and crawled back under the trailer like some broken bitch. Hope the dog doesn't take after the master."

As I was getting warmed up into my enlightening conversation with Amos and hearing my own dialect slip back into redneck twang, his brother, Gunner, slammed the screen door of the trailer. Gunner yelled as he walked toward us. "What's this prissy cock-sucker want, Amos? And why the fuck did he kick Spade?"

"And how are you today, Moon Pie?" I said.

"Don't call me that, Cloud. You know I hate it when people call me that."

"I don't even know if I remember your real name. Folks been callin' you Moon Pie for so long, I just thought that's what your Mama named you."

Gunner never broke stride. He spit a big glob of tobacco juice on the ground and a brown slinky thread of spit fell back against his beard and down the front of his Molly Hatchet T-shirt. He reached behind his back and produced a big Buck knife. Before he got within three steps of me, I stuck the hickory stick out and poked him in the chest, stopping him cold. "You'll be putting that knife away Moon Pie, or I'll take it from you and leave both of you here trying to figure out whose balls are whose."

Amos snarled, reddened with anger and embarrassment. "You prissy muther fucker, you think you gonna whip the both of us?"

"Not if you put your toys away and answer a few questions. 'Course, if you're not of a mind to be cooperative, I could use my stick friend here to give you some incentive," I said with a grin.

Gunner slapped the stick away and lunged at me with the knife. I used the heel of my open palm to smack him just under the nose, right above his upper lip. I grabbed the greasy black hair on the back of his head and spun him to the side so I could get a good bead on Amos. Stepping forward with Gunner in tow, I punted Amos in the crotch. He sunk to the ground face first, lifting a little of the mushy sod with the top of his head as it buried into the ground. I brought my knee up and pulled Gunner's head down at the same time. They collided with a sharp crack and the big man rolled to the mud grabbing his face with both hands. Both men now lay writhing on the ground.

"No respect for southern hospitality," I said. "When you fellas catch your breath, I just have a few questions then I'll leave you two to make up an alternative story as to what just happened."

I walked over to the pickup with the rebel flag glowering at me and looked in the back. There were blocks of wood and chains, all covered with fluffs of dead bird feathers and dried globs of blood. I grabbed two five-gallon buckets and went back to where the boys were now sitting, but still holding their mangled body parts. "Here, why don't you gentlemen take a seat?"

Gunner sat down on a blue Chevron oil bucket, but Amos could only manage to lean his upper body over the top of the other. Amos coughed twice and vomited. It looked like not very well chewed Vienna Sausages.

"Now then, I have only three questions. A cooperative effort on your part will mean my quick departure. If you don't answer or if you lie, I will encourage you with my friend, Old Hickory. Where were you boys last night?"

Amos rasped, "Don't tell this *injun* fucker nothing, brother."

I kicked the bucket out from under Amos and spanked him one good lick on his fat behind. "Amos, *that* is not cooperation. I will ask again. Where were you boys last night?"

Gunner looked up through his parted fingers, blood dripping from his nose. "Shinning deer."

"While I'm not the law, I do believe that is illegal. Where were you shinning the vicious beast?"

"Old man McCullers' place," said Gunner.

"See how cooperative you can be when you try, Moon Pie? You should take heed of your brother there, Amos. Now question number two. Did both of you kill Mr. McCullers' fine prized animal?"

The dogs had eased out from the shadows of the trailer. They were there for back-up, but it seemed a collective decision had been made in their K-9 noodles that back-up wasn't needed yet. Amos pulled himself back onto the bucket and wiped some snot from his scraggly beard. "We ain't shot nothing, don't know nothing about no damn bull."

"Wrong fucking answer, Amos. I believe you fellas need a little more incentive than Old Hickory can provide. I think I have just the thing."

I walked back to the truck and tossed the stick in the cab. Reaching to my own gun rack, I grabbed a cattle prod. I walked back over to the pathetic twins and stuck the prod to Amos's forehead. "Going once, going twice."

"Leave him the fuck alone ya sorry *injun* bastard," said Gunner.

"Name calling, not very hospitable there, Moon Pie. Sticks and stones may break my bones, but a cattle prod will make you cry."

I switched the prod to the lobe of Gunner's right ear and pressed the little white button. A short sizzling sound spat from the end. Gunner shrieked like a cut pig and rolled back onto the mushy earth.

"Which of you two fine marksmen took target practice on Billy the bull?"

"It wasn't us," cried Amos. "We saw a truck parked along the road when we went in the gate, and when we drove out all we saw was that damn bull lying on his side. Somebody else musta shot him. It wasn't us."

"Now that's mighty cooperative there, Amos. Probably not truthful, but cooperative. Question number three. Whose truck was parked by the side of the road?"

"We couldn't see whose goddamn truck it was. It was dark as all hell out there," croaked Gunner.

"There was a full moon last night Moon Pie. I'm sure you could make out some of the details of what the truck looked like."

"We ain't seen nothing," said Amos.

"This is fun, isn't it boys? Just like back in grade school. You boys always picking on the other kids because you failed three grades and were head and shoulders bigger than the rest of us. Now it's just fun as hell seeing you boys dealing with someone your own size. Tell me something about the truck."

I pushed Gunner off the bucket with my foot and put the prod to Amos's forehead again. I thumbed the button and the same sickening sizzle zapped Amos above his one hairy eyebrow. Amos jumped back from the shock and landed in a puddle, splashing mud all over his wife-beater.

"Head lamps," Gunner yelped. "The truck had those big KC lamps bolted to a roll bar over the cab."

"What else?" I said.

"It was blue—dark—and all scratched up on the driver's side," said Gunner.

"We're on a roll now, tell me more."

"Okay, okay. It were Tree's truck," whimpered Amos, struggling to his knees.

"Tree Raulerson?"

"Yeah, it was Tree's truck. Couldn't miss them horns he has mounted to the front like some *Texas* hood ornament."

"Well now, you boys have been mighty helpful. I asked three questions and got three very complete and cooperative answers. Now I can move on and ask that nasty Tree Raulerson some inquiries. I might have to come back and ask some follow up questions. You boys don't mind do you? No, I imagine you got your minds right now and will be much more hospitable in the future. If I do come back, I hope you'll have trained those dogs to respect company a little better. If not, I'll bring my dog training tools with me just in case."

I jumped in the cab of the big diesel and sped off down the lime rock road. In the rear view mirror I could see both brothers giving me the tandem finger.

Chapter 7

Grinding through fourth gear, I spotted the cop lights flashing in my rear view mirror. One-six-eight was visibly painted on the roof of the car. One of the advantages of driving a four-wheel drive is you can see right over the top of most other vehicles. I pulled to a stop under an oak drooping over the side of the road like a hand about to swat a fly. The law enforcer stepped from the car, red haired and muscular. She wore Maui Jim sunglasses, tough but still feminine, the kind that make you wonder, *is she bad or do I just want her to be?* I stepped from the truck just as she reached the tailgate.

"I'll need to see a license for that hog leg you're carrying under your arm there, cowboy," she said.

I smiled and said, "Hell, officer, if you promise to strip search me, I promise I'll resist arrest just enough."

She crinkled her nose and a confident smile crossed her lips. It was Blue, my roommate, lover, and the toughest cop to wear the khaki uniform of the Cable Department of Law Enforcement.

"You're lucky I'm in zone six today. Everyone else on the force would just love to give you a ticket for speeding through our quiet little stretch of the Counties."

I shifted from one foot to the other to shade the sun from my eyes. "Would they give me the ticket because I was speeding or because they were jealous of the fact I bed you amorously and with complete satisfaction on a nightly basis?"

"Listen stud, satisfaction is required, and amorously or not, nightly is a necessity. You solving another of the world's problems today?"

"Afraid so," I replied. "Someone killed old man McCullers' bull, Billy, last night."

"Yeah, I heard."

"So what does the CDLE have to say?"

"Not so fast there, bud. That information is on a need-to-know basis, and right now I'm not so sure the boss needs for you to know."

"What about his and my favorite agent?" I said, flashing my drop-your-pants smile.

"Flattery. I vaguely recognize it. You should practice it more at home and less while trying to swindle information from the boss's favorite agent."

"So you're holding out on me, fine. What's for supper tonight?"

"I don't know—it's Emma's night to cook, so we'll both have to wish for the best and hope she's not feeling experimental."

Emma is Blue's girlfriend.

Whoa big fella… you say to yourself. Then what does that make me? That, my friends, makes me the luckiest man in all of the Cable Counties.

Chapter 8

Emma and Blue were already an item when I first met them a couple of years ago. It started out as a lonely night at Willard's, a backwoods country bar out on County Road 337. I'd stopped by to see my old friend Willard, the owner, to ask him about a case I was working. When I stepped into the soft glow of neon beer signs, I was overcome with manly sexual urges at the sight of these two comely creatures. They were sitting at the bar toasting bottles of Budweiser after throwing back shots of 1800 Tequila. Investigator that I am, I seized the opportunity to search for clues as to why these two would find Willard's an attractive hangout. I forgot what I'd originally come to see Willard about. Emma was tall, five-ten or so, and the redhead was built like my favorite kind of brick house.

Me and the redhead had some history of the official variety some time earlier. "Buy you ladies a drink?" I said, flashing a smile which had launched at least a couple of canoes.

"Sure, cowboy," the redhead said. "But only if you'll saddle up on a stool with us."

Optimism flashed like lightening through my head. *Saddle—oh my—did she say saddle?* I must remember to rub my lucky buckeye seed every day.

"What are you ladies having?"

"Tequila, and chasing it with Bud," the tall one said.

Oh my, I thought, *God does look favorably on the good old country boy.*

"Willard, my good man, three shots of 1800 and three bottles of Budweiser," I called.

Willard, not one for many words, looked sideways out of his one good eye. The patch over the other one covered any emotion either eye might divulge. He lectured, "Boy, you can't tell heifers from bulls. These two ladies are hand-holders; they just want some sucker like you to pay for the lubricant."

"Not tonight Willard," said the redhead. "Tonight we're man hunters. We're looking to see if there is any reason at all to keep you males around."

Did I just walk in the back door of Shangri-La? I thought. I'm a lucky man, but this was over the rainbow even for me. *I will never, ever take you for granted again, my lucky little buckeye seed.*

"Did I just miss something here ladies?" I said.

The red head smoothed curly tendrils of hair behind her ears. "Play your cards right and missing something will be a thing of the past for you, big man."

I fixated on the neon beer sign above the bar. Words. I know there are words one should say in this situation, but search as I might, none would come. Sometimes you just can't get them from brain to tongue.

I finally stammered, "Am I to understand both of you ladies are looking for the same man—a package deal if you would?"

"You got that right, big thunder," said the tall one. "You up for a little game of three-way poker?"

Charm was out the door. Hunger and lust were in the house. "Poker," I said. "As in, times two?"

"That's the name of the game, shoulders," said the red head. "All these other boys were too afraid to even ask, so I guess you're the lucky fella'."

"Oh brother," said Willard as he slid the shots and beer across the bar.

"Shut up, you patch-eyed fool. I might just be their huckleberry," I said, quoting my best Doc Holiday.

"Oh brother," said Willard again.

Blue revealed later they both knew who I was and the seedy language wasn't due to my irresistible maleness, but rather a ploy they discussed employing at the first available opportunity. As I said, I am a lucky man.

That was the first night of our cohabitation and relationship which is now in its second year.

Chapter 9

2001 – Bent Daleen, Dunwoody, Australia

"Benny, when are we gonna settle down and get ourselves hitched? When can we start our own little family?"

"One day Sheila, one day."

"But, when? When will one day come?"

"One day when you least expect it."

"I'm just concerned. You've been here in Dunwoody for going on a year now, and we've been together most of that time. You know I love you, and even though you never say it, I know you love me."

"We're together now and the here and now is the most important thing. Let's just enjoy each other."

"I do enjoy us, here and now. But I want more. When can we make it a little more permanent?"

Bent Daleen reached to the floor beside the bed to a ragged leather backpack. He pulled out a small animal skin pouch and laid it on his bare stomach. Sheila's eyes widened and she felt a momentary hitch in her throat. "What is it Benny? What's in the pouch?"

Daleen slowly opened the strings of the pouch, making seductive eye contact with her. "I reckon now's as good a time as any for us to get started." A small silver bangle dropped from the pouch and landed with a bounce on his flat belly.

"It's a bracelet Benny, an honest to god ring of sorts. Does it mean what I think it means?"

"It means just what you think it means, Sheila."

"Then say it my love. Ask me."

Daleen looked down the bronzed, naked body of the woman. He took a long time surveying the contours of her ample sex. He took her arm and slid the silver bracelet over her hand. "Sheila, my dear, will you marry me?"

For a moment she considered toying with him to seem at least a *little* hard to get. Then she thought better of it and closed in on the kill eagerly. "Yes, Benny. With all my heart and all of my soul, I accept. I will marry you." With the enthusiasm of a puppy she bounced a straddle of Daleen. "Let's christen the moment with a little rough rub, shall we?"

Daleen blinked slowly and with conviction. His expression like that of a predator. "Yes, let's."

He took her, but she did quite a bit of taking herself. Twenty minutes later they lay in heaving gasps on top of sweaty sheets. Her forehead glistened and she fairly hummed with post-coital energy. The physical expression of sex was never satisfying for Daleen, but the power, the feeling of taking something, of subduing someone, was orgasmic in its own right.

"Let's take a bath. I want to wash you. I'll go run the water and light some candles. You bring the radio?"

"Whatever you want, Sheila."

Bent Daleen walked naked into the bathroom and regarded with some remorse the beautiful woman lounging in the bath. He glanced around the small room with rough primitive boards enveloping a footed white porcelain tub. She smiled at him, winked and raised a bubble-coated foot. He returned a long look filled with certainty, yet not warm in any way. Her face ticked for a moment as she tried to decipher his unusual body language.

Daleen plugged the radio into an outlet. He turned and faced her, the radio still dangling from his hand. Sheila said, "Come on Benny, put the radio on something soothing and join me. I have some wild lavender soap I've been saving for a special occasion."

Daleen leaned in towards her, kissing her forehead, then took a step back.

"Sheila my dear, the earth is large, but make no mistake, it is a culture of one. Its resources are not so infinite, as much of the common population would have us believe. It does not have space to waste on the weak of mind, body, or spirit."

She crinkled her forehead at such an unromantic statement at such a romantic time.

He clicked his tongue and tossed the radio into the tub. The porcelain sea boiled momentarily with electricity and the girl's thrashing spasms of agony.

When she was still, he unplugged the radio. Grasping her lifeless arm, he looked into her dead, shocked eyes bobbing above the bubbles. He removed the bracelet and placed it on his own hairy wrist.

***

An hour later Bent Daleen appeared in the doorway of the old church at the center of the small rural town of Dunwoody. A town meeting had been called to discuss the recent deaths of hundreds of sheep. The farmers were at their wit's end to discover the cause of the huge losses.

The entire township filled the pews. All eighty-four inhabitants of Dunwoody, every man, woman, and child were present. This was a serious problem requiring the whole community to band together.

An old woman noticed him in the doorway and smiled in greeting. A farmer acknowledged him with a slight wave. "So good to see you, Benny. Where's your Sheila?"

Daleen took a moment to finish his head count. Satisfied, he looked into the eyes of the old woman and said, "She's in the tub, needed to clean herself." She gave him a knowing glance and returned her attention to the speaker at the pulpit.

Daleen stepped deftly backwards into the darkness and closed the doors of the chapel. He walked to a dusty Land Rover and started its engine.

At the edge of town Daleen fished a small black plastic box from his coat pocket. He rubbed the outer casing and let his finger linger on the single button. He adjusted the rear view mirror to see the lights glowing from the church spire.

He pressed the button and watched, smiling, as everyone in Dunwoody who had seen the face of Bent Daleen exploded upward into the night sky.

***

2003 – Santao, Argentina
A village that successfully farmed goats for centuries becomes a ghost town.

2006 – Seoul, South Korea
The state-run poultry plant is shut down because all the birds are found to have contracted a rare skin disease contagious to humans.

2009 – Helmand Province, Afghanistan
Hundreds of U.S. Marines fighting in the Afghan War find themselves stricken with a mysterious illness affecting their respiratory system causing extreme fatigue.

The list of successful operations Bent Daleen commanded grew in number and severity. The Center for Disease Control in Atlanta, Georgia tracked and studied each of the holocausts on animals and people, but could never establish a link. Every time, a form of biological warfare was introduced into the local ecosystem, but the strain or virus was always different.

In 2011, after completing an assignment in the Indian Ocean with a virus collapsing the immune system of tuna, Daleen was recalled back to the Institute and underwent a further, advanced series of engineering therapies to finally prepare him for the United States. His classes focused on politics, religion, and on how to blend into America's capitalistic society. He excelled in the religious training.

Bent Daleen was now the Arch Angel, equipped to destroy with a belief that he did it for God—with a violence which had no parallel.

Chapter 10

The Cable Counties, Florida

I was woken the next morning when, very early, Blue was called out. I was surprised when she told me, as she was getting dressed, it was a murder. We don't have much in the way of unnatural dying in the Cable Counties. Then, before she left, Blue took a call about another bull killing—this time two animals. With murder on Blue's mind, I figured it was worth taking a look for myself. It might be awhile before the law got to caring about dead cattle again.

The site of the killings made me cringe. It was the Ford Ranch. I had a history with the owner. It wasn't pleasant or endearing.

Dawn was breaking as I drove toward Ford's ranch. I got a call from MacGregor Knox.

"Cloud, there's been another bull killed."

"Yeah, I know. Why are you calling me so eager and early with the news?"

"I've been reactivated. Got a call from the Governor himself. The Commission ain't gonna be too happy about that."

"Screw'em. Blue said there was a body—a human body."

"That's why the Gov called me, I reckon."

"I'll be there in five minutes."

***

Knox was standing with a few of the Cable Counties' finest when I arrived. He gave them instructions and they all hurried off. I waited until he was alone.

"You got any idea's *now*?" I asked.

He gave me his patented 'fuck you' smile. "Some are forming as we speak."

"Sure doesn't sound like anyone from around here."

"No, it doesn't. *You* got any ideas?"

"The frustrated hunter scenario doesn't seem plausible. I spoke with the Gallagher boys. They lied to me quite a bit, but I don't think they're anywhere near smart enough to pull this off. Also, they're ornery, but I don't think they're people killers."

"Yeah, Gallaghers are mean, but I don't peg them for this. Who're you talking to next?"

"After Rufus?"

"I figured he was next on your list, but yeah, after him."

"Tree Raulerson."

"Christ, Cloud, he's just this side of retarded. You're moving down the intellectual scale."

I shrugged. "He's not retarded; he just acts that way for show. Besides, I'm just shaking things up."

Knox shook his head. "I've seen you find way too many needles in way too many haystacks to give you shit, but I think you're wasting your time with Raulerson."

Chapter 11

The Ford Ranch was named Black Prong. Way back before he bought the place, it was a hunting camp stretching out over nearly two thousand acres.

Rufus "Pappy" Ford was a hard man; one I knew from my high school days when I dated his daughter Daisy for one splendid summer. He probably didn't like me any more now than he did back then. He figured I was bent on deflowering his Daisy. Little did he know I was a few people back in line from that particular honor.

Black Prong was an immaculate ranch. High, black board fences were always kept in perfect repair. Huge limestone rocks marked the entry to the long paved drive leading to a big colonial house. The rocks had the Black Prong brand engraved on them, a trident with the letters B and P engraved in the center of each prong. Ford was the only rancher in Cable who primarily bred and raised bulls, rather than cattle. What little research I'd done so far told me he was also the only one who'd been so unfortunate as to have two bulls killed. I was sure this would have put him in a near permanent bad mood.

Ford sat on the tailgate of his truck, alone. I went to the back of my truck and let Jack and Jake out. The dogs immediately began to canvas the yard, marking each and every plant, rock, and tire they could find. Ford was whittling a large branch, skinning the bark off the sides. It looked like he was making his own Louisville Slugger. This wasn't what I wanted to see.

As I approached Rufus, I thought, *I'm the one walking softly. He's the one whittling a very big stick*. He didn't look up, but I knew he'd already seen me coming a mile away. Ford was one of those very aware people who, because of the solitude he lives in, always knows exactly what's happening in his surroundings.

When I got close, I chose the humble approach and said, when he finally looked at me, "Mr. Ford."

He was smoking a cigar. It bobbed in his clenched teeth when he spoke. "Jeremiah."

We looked at each other for a very uncomfortable couple of moments. Then he said, "You're a nervy one aren't you, boy? Didn't figure on ever seeing you on my land again after that night I asked you to leave."

"The shotgun you were holding at the time made your point. I wouldn't be here for a social call."

His grin clenched and I could see the word *social* meant more than I had intended. He looked back at his whittling and said, "What do you want?"

"I've been asked by Ben McCullers to look into the bull deaths around here. Since I know you're one of the victims I figured on asking you a few questions and maybe have a look at where your bulls were killed. I assumed you wouldn't mind me coming out here, since my intent was to help out."

"You assume a lot, Cloud."

"Well, will you talk to me about the bulls?"

"You say old Ben asked you?

"I know him pretty well."

"Yeah? Does he know *you* all that well?" Dripping sarcasm.

"Maybe this was a bad idea, maybe I'll go and talk to some of the other ranchers."

"No, I've been wanting to ask you some questions of my own for quite a spell. We're having rocky mountain oysters for supper, so maybe you can stay."

Rocky mountain oysters are bull testicles, deep-fried after being heavily battered in corn meal. Bad as they sound, they're absolutely divine. "Thank you for the invitation. I'd be honored."

"I know you've been back two or three years. Where were you the dozen or so years before that?"

"The Army."

"That's not what I heard. I heard it was something a bit more."

"People talk gossip."

"Sometimes gossip don't turn out to be untrue."

"Well, Mr. Ford, I was in the Army."

"Why'd you quit? You get hurt or was it that you just couldn't commit, like so many other things in your life?"

I knew he was more than hinting at my short-lived relationship with his Daisy. I wanted to tell him I was young, running on testosterone, and Daisy was easy. But I kept those comments to myself.

"I just got tired of playing a *game* for a living. Some people think that sounds kinda snotty or ungrateful for the talents I was given, but it's the truth. Besides, if I stayed longer, I might have turned out to be as evil as some people think." I said the last while looking at the craggy profile of a tired, bitter man, who despite all that happened between us before, deep down still really wanted to like me.

The old man accepted the olive branch and decided to ease up on the prickly jabs. I knew he wasn't finished by any stretch, but maybe he would answer a few questions first.

"What can you tell me about your bulls getting killed?"

"Let's go for a ride. I'll show you where the kills happened."

I was sure this meant we were going in his truck, but instead of opening the door, he reached in through the open driver's window and pulled what looked like a garage door opener from the visor and clipped it to his belt. Then he walked over to the passenger side of my truck and got in. I took the hint. I opened the tailgate and whistled. Jake and Jack bolted from an interesting pile of garden hose they were taking turns marking. With effortless grace, they did a twin hop, step, and jump and both ten-inch tall dogs landed on the tailgate some three feet above the ground.

Sometimes when I'm alone with the dogs I'll unload them and whistle again just so I can watch their gymnastics. It always makes me smile. I gave the dogs a stay command and got into the cab.

Ford was flipping the visor up after attaching the small device. I wanted to ask what it was, but I also wanted to seem cool like I already knew, so I kept quiet. He pointed to a stretch of black top winding up a small grade to a long pole barn. It was a feedlot where he fed young bulls high-calorie growth feed until they were ready to be sold. Ford's operation had grown considerably since I was here during high school. He'd obviously done rather well. Everything was big, immaculately clean, and had a high tech feel.

The smell of manure in the feedlot was almost overwhelming. I'm a country boy, but being in the middle of a barn where hundreds of animals are doing their business was suffocating. I saw Ford looking at me and almost made out a grin. My eyes were on the verge of watering. Finally, I couldn't restrain my thoughts. "This smells like the ass-end of Noah's Ark."

The old man gave a small cluck. "Smells like money to me."

The barn was open on all sides with a tin roof cover. It was sectioned off into square holding pens by thick cable fencing on metal poles. It was amazing to see such efficiency within an industry not known for streamlining.

The air in the cab of the truck was thick with pride. Ford was fairly glowing. I figured the best way to get the information and cooperation I needed was to flatter him a bit. "How many bulls do you run through here?"

"We run through about a thousand head of our own every year. On top of that, we buy bulls from other ranchers and feed them, give them their shots, and generally mother them until they're ready to sire—so probably another thousand."

"I had no idea your operation was so large."

"Biggest one of its kind. Not everything is bigger in Texas."

We left the barn and drove into a kind of cul-de-sac. At the far end was a wrought iron gate. I was beginning to slow in front of the gate, wondering if I was going to have to get out and open the gate or if the big boss man would lower himself to such a task. Instead, Ford reached up to the device clipped to the visor. The gate automatically began to swing open. The surprise showed on my face, giving away my lack of coolness. Rufus looked at me and smiled. "Twenty-first century and all," he said.

The gate opened into a large prairie, maybe three hundred acres, bordered on the back by a large stand of pines and oaks. On the far right was a broad pond, maybe even a lake. It was absolutely beautiful. Me, living here in the same county most of my life, and I hadn't ever noticed.

"This whole prairie was under water when I bought the place. I got the land for a song, because everyone thought it was a swamp that could never undergo reclamation. I drained the prairie and built a dyke around the whole thing. There's a pump in that tin shack over by the lake. We can pull water off when it rains too much and pump water from the lake back to the prairie when times are dry. Very *green*, not that I give a damn."

We moved at a slow idle around the dyke. It was roughly ten feet high and sloped steeply down on both sides. I had to pay attention to make sure we stayed on the narrow road following the crest of the dyke. I found my eyes wandering at several points and had to remind myself of the road. Ford never said a word. He seemed to be in some zen-like trance. A large bald eagle left a nest built in the top of a thirty-foot pine tree that had been struck by lightning. The eagle soared over the lake just fifty yards or so to our left and dove toward the water. The powerful wings hitched once, then again, lifting the eagle from the surface with a large-mouth bass, maybe two pounds, in its talons. The majestic bird circled back toward the nest.

I remembered my driving and jerked the truck back into the ruts atop the dyke.

On the far side of the lake was another small prairie and then State Road 121. A sudden sense of morose fell over Pappy Ford, and I could tell he was still mourning the loss of his bulls. He lifted a scarred hand and pointed to a concrete mineral trough about a hundred yards from the road. "Head over toward the trough. That's where they killed Zeus, the first one."

I shifted the truck into four-wheel drive and drove off the bank of the dyke. The kill spot was staked with a post; a sheet-metal wreath was attached. *This man feels like one of his kids was killed, not just a bull*, I thought to myself.

Chapter 12

Pappy Ford bent down and cupped a handful of sand near the base of the post. He spread his fingers and let the sand trickle between them. He looked toward the lake and heaved a sigh. "Zeus was the third bull killed, counting the ones in Levy and Marion Counties. He was also the most valuable killed overall. That's until they killed Billy the other night."

"I'm sure Zeus had great sentimental value, but how much was he worth?"

"Zeus was a pure sire, used to breed our purebred Angus cows. He was also a donor, a bull they take semen from and freeze for artificial insemination. I reckon he made the ranch about a hundred thousand dollars a year on his own. He had maybe another five or six years left before he started to shoot blanks, so Zeus was probably a million-dollar bull."

"A million-dollar bull," I said with genuine awe. I had no idea a bull could be worth so much and produce such valuable sperm.

I didn't see any tears, but the old man pulled a red handkerchief from his back pocket and blew his nose. As uncomfortable as this was, I was on a roll. I asked, "And you say Billy was even more valuable?"

"Ben McCullers probably doesn't even know how valuable Billy was. Billy single-handedly kept his farm in the black for several years now. He was a big time donor. I don't rightly know what old Ben will do now without Billy. All my prized stock is insured, but old Ben didn't know anything about insurance, or he was just too stubborn to pay for it. He'll probably scrape by for a few years, but that farm of his ain't worth shit without Billy."

"Do you know if any of the other bulls killed were anywhere near as valuable?"

"Most of the other bulls weren't worth even a tenth of that amount. Only one other was in the million-dollar range."

"Which one?"

"My other one killed last night, Apollo."

I put my hand to my forehead, not as much to shade the sun as to make some gesture, while I considered the gravity and sheer dollar amounts I'd just been handed. A possible three million dollars in bulls had been killed on two ranches alone. The others probably added up to another million lost. The loss of four million dollars' worth of prime assets in such a small area provided a motive I hadn't previously considered.

Ford seemed to gather his emotions and said, "Let's head back toward the house and I'll show you where Apollo was killed."

We drove around the far side of the lake. "Do you have any idea why these bulls were killed or who might be behind it?" I asked.

Ford rubbed leathery hands over his face and looked out the window. "At first I thought, like everybody else, some sorry-ass hunters were responsible. But *this* has got to be more than that. Mac said the person killed last night was the second this year. Somebody with a real agenda is killing these people, bulls too. If we keep losing them at this rate, several of the farms in Cable will be out of business. Someone could be after the land, but it seems more of a statement to me. I'm not sure someone isn't trying to make a point."

"What point might that be?"

"Well, it could be the environmentalists. They're pretty riled up about the manure run-off all the farms in the area produce. They say it contaminates drinking water and the underground springs that supply the swamps. Or it could be the animal rights bunch. They come around about once a year and make trouble for the ranchers with the media, always talking about the inhumane treatment of the livestock."

"Sounds like you wouldn't mind them ending up with the blame, but you really don't think it was them. Either of them, I mean."

"I don't, and that's the bitch of it. I wish it were as easy as that. But I'll be damned if I really know who's behind all this."

"Anyone you might have pissed off lately?"

"Hell, you know I don't much give a damn what people think, so I'm sure there're a few."

"You fire anyone lately?"

"People come and go in this business. Ranch work is hard and most of these local country boys think they want to be cowboys, but they got their idea of what it's like from television. 'Bout six months back I did have to fire the Gallagher boys. Caught them stealing. But you know they don't have the brains between them to pull off killing these bulls *and* the humans, let's not forget."

"No one else you can think of?"

"Well, there was this one other fella' came around about a year ago. Kinda strange, asking all kinds of questions about the cattle industry. Said he was interested in getting into the business. But he seemed too *city*, maybe even foreign. I ended up asking him to leave, 'bout the same way I asked you that night with Daisy."

"With a shotgun?"

The old man looked over at me and blinked, then looked back toward his window. I figured this meant the gun *did* make an appearance.

Chapter 13

As the truck idled along, I began to feel a kinship with Rufus Ford I'd never felt before. He seemed to be a man of high integrity who'd worked hard to make something of his ranch, and now he saw it threatened. I sensed he was at the breaking point—when men take things into their own hands.

"I'm actually pretty glad Ben hired you. This thing has gotten out of hand, and if everyone doesn't stop farting around and someone doesn't start figuring things out, I'm gonna get a little more involved. It's not just the money, you understand. It's the threat. I'm not gonna see a life's work fade out because some asshole with something to prove has a bug up his ass."

I kept looking forward, but felt obliged to comment, "I probably can't identify with the loss, but I believe exactly as you do about the threat."

"Do you believe in God, Cloud?"

Oh my, there it was, the question that crashed a thousand potential relationships. I usually won't comment on the subject. It never gets me anywhere. But the man seemed to be asking for himself, not as an interview question for me. "The short answer is yes," I said.

"What's the long answer?"

"Mr. Ford, I'm not sure this conversation will help me find out who killed your bulls."

"Call me Rufus or Ford, and I didn't ask you about God to help find the killer."

"I'm not sure my answer will endear me, not that we've had a past where

48

that has happened."

"I'm a man who doesn't have many friends. It's not that I couldn't, I just don't enjoy the company of many people. I spend most all of my time with employees, my family, and the animals. Every once in a while I get hungry for some intelligent input. You're right, we've had our differences, but I think I would like to know your opinion."

We pulled up to another gate at the far end of the lake and Ford again pushed the magic button on his little box. The gate swung open and we drove on through. A burrowing sand owl was sitting on a fence post. It was skinning a small animal, maybe a rat. The owl held the animal firmly against the top of the post and used its beak to tear the tough hide of the victim. The owl looked at us to measure the threat. He fluffed his wings a couple of times in an offensive gesture and considered abandoning the animal. In the rear view mirror I saw the owl watch us awhile, then continue his skinning.

I took a deep breath. "I believe in God, but it probably should begin with a small 'g'. It's easier to explain what I think he, or *it*, is not. I don't believe in a third party entity. I don't believe there's someone out there watching our every move and judging our righteous behavior. I don't believe sin is as simple as we've made it out to be. And I don't believe Heaven or hell is an actual place where the believers or the damned spend eternity. I do believe there is a scorecard and everything counts."

"It seems you may have lost your faith at some point."

"Not at all. I believe the Bible is a very informative book that gives us many concepts to live by. For instance, you said faith. The Bible says if you have faith, even in such small amounts as to compare it to a grain of mustard seed, you can move mountains. When I was a kid, I thought this meant wishing, and that if you wished hard enough, the mountain would just get up and jump. But later when I actually saw a mountain, I began to believe faith was action. That a man or group of men could move a mountain. They just had to use bulldozers and earthmovers. I drove through dynamited passes and saw where men *had* moved mountains. So I think I believe in *faith* more than most other concepts, but with a focused human spirit."

"That's why I asked. I knew you'd have an interesting answer." With that the old man looked back out his window and the conversation on that topic was closed.

Up ahead and close to the barn was an identical post and wreath. Ford pointed silently toward it, and I turned the truck in that direction.

In comparing the two sites, the only thing I immediately saw they had in common was they were both close to county roads. The killers didn't have to invade the property very far before they could surprise the bulls. This fact didn't help much—and probably hurt in that it made more sense that frustrated hunters could have done the deed from the road. We didn't get out of the truck this time, just stopped momentarily. Then Rufus said, "Let's get on to the house, it's supper time."

Supper was an outdoor affair. About fifty employees and various family members decked out in their best cowboy and cowgirl attire gathered under two century oaks. Feeling like a party crasher, I was thinking up an excuse when Ford opened the door, got out, and leaned against the front. I didn't see any options. I got out and joined him. He looked toward the sky and took a cigar from a breast pocket. It looked as if it were used, a couple of times. He lit it with a match and blew a blue cloud towards the darkening sky.

Then Ford looked at me. "You probably thought I was going to grill you about the Daisy thing. Maybe you were right, maybe I was, but even an old dog can learn a thing or two. Come on over and have some supper, then you get your ass to the business of finding out who killed my bulls. If you need anything while you're hunting the bastards down, and I do mean *anything*, you give me a call."

I followed Pappy Ford to a table covered in a red and white-checkered tablecloth and laden with every delight of country cuisine. I stood in line and served myself helpings of everything that would fit. When finished with the line I proceeded over to a giant pot settled over an open fire, where a man was deep frying the mountain oysters. I used another bowl I'd snagged from the table to serve myself a sizeable portion of the rare, southern delicacy.

I was relieved to find supper uneventful. I met and spoke with many of the people, but it was mostly small-talk about life on the ranch. A few asked me about being a detective and at least a dozen asked about my life in the

Army. I found no clues about the bull killers. Finally, I bid farewell to the group and thanked Ford and his misses for the chow. Then I was back in my truck, heading home the long way.

Thinking time.

Chapter 14

The next day I was in my truck heading back toward town. It was nearly eleven and only an hour until I could have lunch without feeling guilty. I decided to go and have a talk with Tree Raulerson. This would push lunch back, which wasn't my custom. *Oh the sacrifices we good guys make.*

Tree Raulerson lived on the south side of town. He wasn't a member of the welcoming committee for our small community. My lingering memory of Tree was from a domestic disturbance issue I helped his wife with a year or so before. It didn't go well for Tree, and it was the last chapter in a rocky relationship, which ended in divorce. I hoped Tree had forgotten and would settle for some mature conversation. I was sorely disappointed.

Tree goes about six eight and is as big and broad as he is tall. He was standing in his yard skinning a pig hanging from a branch. As I approached, he acted as if he didn't know I was there. Grabbing a garden hose, he began spraying the bloody carcass.

"How're you doing there, Tree," I said, standing just behind him.

"The fuck you want, Cloud?"

I sized him up. "I just want to ask you some questions about a bull killed over at Mr. McCullers' place."

"Don't know nothing 'bout no bull," Tree said, never taking his eyes from the dangling pig.

"C'mon Tree, you must have seen something or maybe done something."

"You callin' me a liar, you skinny fuck?"

I'm not a small man, about six-three or so. But this wasn't something I was looking forward to.

Before things got any worse, we both turned to see a CDLE cruiser pull into the yard. I was as relieved as I can remember. Blue got out the car and was talking into the portable radio clipped to her lapel. She stopped, picked up the garden hose, and kinked it.

"Gentlemen," she said.

Tree didn't mind stomping my backside, but I believe he was truly scared of Blue.

He dropped the hose and turned to face her. "Agent."

Blue looked at me, then aimed her question between us. "What we got going on here, Tree?"

"This sorry fucker, s'cuse my language, Blue, is accusing me of killin' some bull."

"*Did* you kill the bull, Tree?"

"Wouldn't kill somebody's pet. Real men hunt wild things," Tree said, his eyes never leaving the ground. "Billy was already dead when I stopped on the side of the road. I stop there every other day or so and feed him a couple of carrots and maybe a sugar cube through the fence. I wouldn't ever shoot such a beautiful thing. I loved that bull like he was my own. I seen somebody else though." He raised his head, and I could see his eyes go sharp with hate.

"Who did you see?"

"'Bout ten freaky-looking spooks were out there," Tree said.

From Tree, "Spooks" could mean black people. He wasn't a racist; he just didn't know the difference. Probably never heard the term *politically correct*. I couldn't resist the urge to butt in. "You mean you saw black folk out there, or by *spooks* do you mean ghosts killed Billy then cut his ears and tail off?"

With an obvious snarl, Tree turned to the pig hanging from the limb. He didn't seem too keen on answering any questions from me.

Blue stared hard at Tree, and he could feel it. "Well Tree, how 'bout it? You saying it was ghosts?"

"Weren't no niggers. Ghosts neither. They was people all right. But they was all dressed up in olive drab green camo. One guy had a purple lightning bolt with a big slice-a moon 'cross his chest."

"How was it you got such a good look at them?" Blue asked.

"I shined them with my spot light. You would've thought I turned the power of God loose on them. They all ran to the road and jumped in a van parked on the edge of the woods. They was all screaming, and half of them fell down a couple of times on their way. One of them was running in a circle until another one grabbed him and hustled him off towards the van. Bunch of crazy hippies or something, ya ask me."

"Why didn't you call me or the sheriff?"

"Exactly 'cos of this right here. I figured nobody would believe me and would probably figure I was the one who kilt Billy."

"You recognize any of them?" I asked.

Again, Tree looked back toward the pig. He was doing his level best to ignore me.

Blue pressed him, "Did you recognize any of them?"

"No. Didn't see no faces. One of them was carrying a stick with a hook on the end though."

"Like a meat hook?"

"No, like one of them sticks them guys herd sheeps carry."

"You see any other interesting things like that?" Blue said, flattering him.

"No, that's about it."

"You done real good, Tree. I appreciate how cooperative you've been. You're a fine fella," said Blue.

I looked at her like she'd just stepped from an alien spacecraft, but she ignored me. Tree walked over to a patch of sunlight seeping between the branches of the big oak trees and pulled three, then two more, wild flowers from the ground. He turned and moved toward us, snapping the roots off the flowers. The big man walked up to Blue and turned his head away like the big, dumb animal he was, while at the same time offering the flowers to her.

Blue said, "Thanks Tree, that's real sweet of you."

Tree shrugged his enormous shoulders and went back to the water hose.

"I hope they try to resist arrest or something when you go to get 'em. Nobody should kill such a fine thing as Billy," said Tree.

"You willing to write all that down?" Blue said.

"Can't write," Tree said, embarrassed. "I'll sign my name to a paper you write that says the same though."

Blue looked at me and I nodded. She went to her car to get the paperwork and the hose immediately jumped to life. Tree started spraying the pig carcass as if all this hadn't happened.

"I wish she hadn't pulled up when she did," Tree said, facing the pig.

"Why's that?" I asked.

"Bull or no bull, I been a waitin' for some excuse to stomp your skinny ass for a long time."

I *was* very glad Blue arrived when she did.

Chapter 15

"Well, what do you think?" Blue asked, as we leaned against her patrol car.

"I think Tree is sweet on you."

"I'm a mighty sweet lady. Can't blame Tree if he has good taste."

"You know anything about some gang of hippies roaming the country side in Vietnam-era camouflage, killing innocent livestock *and* people to boot, I might add?"

"No," she said, a little frustrated. "You might just have to put your cape on for this one, superhero. The boss's going to be busy hunting the murderer. He isn't likely to pursue the bull killer portion of this cluster fuck on the information I've gathered. He knows the good citizens around here would rather pretend that ghostly, camouflaged bull killers are a figment of somebody's imagination."

"And you?"

"I'll help you all I can, but as you know, I serve at the pleasure of the Agent-In-Charge."

"By the way, where did you get the notion to follow this up with Tree?"

"I was out at Mr. McCullers' place asking him who he'd seen on or around his place over the past few weeks. He said he'd run the Gallagher boys off the night before and seen Tree on many occasions slipping something through the fence to Billy. He said the bull always walked to the fence whenever he would see Tree's truck pull up, so he always figured Tree to be giving Billy a treat of some kind. Guess the man is just a harmless animal lover."

That pissed me off with Ben. I knew he'd been holding back. But he, like all men, succumbed to Blue's feminine wiles.

"Yeah? Whadda ya think that pig hanging up there would have to say about that?"

"Well I believe ole Tree. He and I seem to have made a connection. He doesn't seem to care much for you though. Why you reckon that is?"

"He's just jealous of my manliness, my truck, my social life, my ability to write, or maybe he's still pissed off about the divorce."

"You're a strange guy, Cloud."

"Unique, some people would say."

"I have to make a call to Mac, update him on what I've found out today. What're you going to do? Actually, don't tell me. I think it might be better if I didn't know."

"You're probably right. But right this minute I'm going for some lunch. Want to join me?"

"Thanks, but I'm meeting Emma for lunch. Besides, you're probably not heading for the healthy side of the trough."

"I'll see you at home tonight."

"Emma and I have tickets to *The Dancing Lad* over at the Cross Town Theatre. We didn't figure you'd be interested."

"You figured right. You ladies have a nice time."

"Maybe a movie at home before we go?"

"Sounds good."

Blue got into her squad car and I hurried to leave myself. No need to provoke Tree by being on his land without a law officer handy.

Chapter 16

At around eight-thirty the movie was over and an acre or two of popcorn had met its match. Emma and Blue headed to Gainesville for their rendezvous with *The Dancing Lad*. I went to the leather recliner sitting on the back deck. The deck was entirely enclosed in folding glass doors and looked out over six thousand acres of beautiful Lake Santa Fe.

Lightning bugs lit up the outside and danced in the shadow of a fountain spraying from the center of a rock cove. I'd built the cove with the intention of never having to leave home to fish. But after being back in Cable for a year or so, I learned how to fly a floatplane and fishing locations took on a whole new geography.

Settling into the recliner with my laptop, I typed notes of what I'd learned so far about the case. I called up the online address of the Cattlemen's Association and emailed the notes to Tom Goodrich. Then I pulled up a central state map and looked at the Cable Counties area. I made a grid around the area and pasted it to a separate file. I consulted the notes Goodrich gave me and placed a red dot on each location where a bull was killed. I triangulated the center of the map and looked at the area closest to the center of the killings. On the map, it initially looked like a very benign configuration.

While the triangulation was underway a thought occurred to me. I was following up on leads having something to do with "good" people. Whoever did this was not a "good" person. I was going to have to start following up with some of the people on the fringe to see if they could give me some information about the kinds of characters I should be hunting.

The computer beeped, signaling a completed mission. If I hadn't been a little wild in my youth, I wouldn't have remembered the location it came up with at all. But such was not the case. I recognized the out-of-the-way intersection as the Old County-Line Bar and Grill, an establishment that burned down many years ago. But on its ashes, The Construction Site, a seedier kind of place where many of my fellow youths and I lost our virginity, was built. The Construction Site was a whorehouse. It was country, mean, and not a place for romance. When one went looking for the Valley of Death fearing no evil, one went to The Construction Site.

I called the dogs, telling them we were going for a ride. The night was not young. I was far passed any inclination to seek sex, drugs, or rock and roll, but the Site was where I headed for my next crop of answers.

***

There was something more going on than just some local, frustrated hunters killing bulls. It seemed someone or group of someones had a more far-reaching agenda. The people-killing was a big hint but not a clincher. This wasn't what the Cable Counties were all about. This was from outta town.

The whorehouse was not able to advertise its true intent, since prostitution is illegal in all parts of the state. Nevertheless, everyone knew the real business being conducted at The Construction Site was the selling of flesh.

Just over the Alachua/Levy County line, a hand-painted sign said The Construction Site was just a mile and a half down a common country road. I felt a familiar clench in my gut telling me trouble worth getting into was close at hand.

I swung the truck into a gravel parking lot far too immense to service such an out-of-the-way bar. I put the dogs in the back of the pickup where their mobile "condo" took up about a third of the bed. The Sheba cats of ancient Egypt didn't live as well as Jake and Jack. Their "moms" demanded that if I insisted on taking them with me during "life threatening" chases and cases, they were to be treated like kings. I grudgingly gave in, even though in my own mind I really wanted the dogs to be comfortable, just like me.

Flashing barricades lead from the parking lot to the front door, which wasn't a door at all, but a wire gate with "Caution Keep Out" signs attached. The bouncers acting as bookends outside the gate were dressed in denim overalls, shirtless, and had a red handkerchief around their massive necks and yellow hard-hats embossed with the words "Construction Site Security."

One of the bookends collected a ten-dollar cover charge, which I expected. The other bouncer led me down a hallway made of concrete girders with rebar showing through broken crevices. I boarded an expanded metal elevator cage at the end of the hall and bid farewell to my security escort.

A huge *something* opened the opposite door of the cage. In all the years I visited the Site, I'd never known whether this was a man or just hair covering a garbage truck. He handed me a fluorescent yellow card and pointed to a sign reading "four-drink minimum." He spoke no words and made no sound.

I walked into what truly looked to be a room under construction. Unfinished walls led to exposed wires and two-by-fours at odd angles. The lights were blue/black and shown from caged work lamps hanging haphazardly from the open ceiling. Steam rose from the center of the room and reflected a pulsing orange light slashing the dark room.

The bar itself was a workbench with vices holding menus at three chair intervals. Scaffolding was rigged around the room — draped with the women dancing and contorting to the music. The girls were surprisingly beautiful and scantily clad in the same denim overalls as the bouncers. Underneath, they wore white wife-beater t-shirts with many rips and tears. Some of the overalls were worn so thin they became translucent with each pulse of the orange light, others were cut off very short, barely allowing the imagination a chance.

I found an unoccupied table, which was actually a huge steel cable spool. As rough as it looked at first, the high-back leather mini-recliners surrounding the spool brought back the feel of top-shelf.

Twin waitresses appeared—and I do mean real twins, who were waitresses. Blond hair ran halfway down their backs over sleeveless flannel work shirts tied at the waist. They wore khaki painter's pants and work belts filled with bar supplies instead of tools.

Twin number one didn't ask what I wanted, but instead told me there were only five drinks served at The Construction Site:

- The Loaded Thermos = Cable's answer to a Long Island Iced Tea
- The Claw Hammer = Cable's answer to a Whiskey Sour
- The Feathered Screw Driver = Grey Goose Vodka and Orange Juice
- The Rusty Rivet = A dirty, tequila laden mystery
- The Circuit Overload = Bartender's mood

I was the good customer and ordered the Thermos.

Before they left, one of them pulled out what appeared to be a blueprint of some kind, unrolled it in front of me, and set a pair of wire cutters on each end. They turned in synchronicity and headed for the bar.

On each page of the plan was a color, poster-size picture of a scaffold dancer with a miniature bio including measurements, age, hobbies, what city they were from, likes and dislikes, and a code name.

Page one was a sweaty outdoor picture of a woman bent over at the waist, looking over her shoulder as she pulled on a large wrench attached to a chrome pipe. She was wearing an orange mesh reflective vest over nothing else, and high cut-off denim shorts. Her code name was "Earth Mover."

On the second page was a full layout of a beautiful redhead leaning against a large tire. She was wearing khaki overalls with no shirt, which let me peak at the dark areolas under the straps. She was obviously on break with a black lunch box opened at her side, complete with plaid thermos. She was about to take a bite of a submarine sandwich. Her code name was "Front End Loader."

The remaining three pages featured equally beautiful women with names connected to the construction trade.

I returned my attention to the room. I'm a detective of sorts, so I detected.

I recognized a few faces around the bar. They turned away when they saw me looking in their direction. Everyone was aware of the gossip that could start around town if you were seen at the Site. The majority of the people in the place were strangers, and this was odd. I remembered a time when I was younger, I would have known just about every soul.

My drink arrived and I took that first "all feeling" pull from the glass tumbler. The rich whiskey, warm and full of possibilities, slid down my throat. As I looked over the rim of my glass, Cannery Row, the Madame of the Site, who I'd known most of my adult life, sashayed over to my table. Cannery went about three hundred pounds, but *was*, in my estimation, a beautiful woman. She was probably in her sixties by now, but you couldn't tell from the energy the big woman exuded.

"Well, well, well. If it isn't my little *Storm Cloud*."

I stood and pulled one of the mini recliners back from the spool. My eyes met the Madame's. I felt a motherly reflection. "Cannery," I said with appropriate gentlemanly charm.

She said, "I been working here in one job or another for going on thirty years and *you* are the only male soul who's ever pulled my chair out each and every time I come to the table. If we're not careful, people will begin to talk."

"Considering our respective reputations, the talking most people would do might only do us some good," I said, flashing a wry smile.

She threw her head back and bellowed laughter that would make Santa himself jealous. The Twins returned, a little tentative—a couple of servants making sure the grand high mistress was given the appropriate attention. Cannery grabbed an armful of each of the girls and together the three of them looked like a giant cookie that had too little wafer and too much filling. "These here are named Jane and Joan, but we just call them 'Ditto.' Ladies, this here is Cloud, the ripest peach in the grove. My *love*, if I were but twenty years younger."

The girls giggled obediently, and I could see I'd grown ten feet tall in their estimation. Cannery gave the girls a double fanny pat. "Bring us a bottle."

The girls hurried to get the mistress's bidding fast, bumping into each other in their eagerness.

"Well I reckon you aren't here for the scenery or the pickins'. I know you're all set up with two honey's which, by the way, I always knew it would take more than one woman, even a full size woman, to take care of you. What's the latest?"

"What do you hear about bulls, dead bulls?"

She looked uncharacteristically shocked. "Oh lord, sweet love, you found yourself all tied up in that mess?"

"Afraid so."

"Well, you're asking in the right place, but it's a mighty dangerous question to be asking."

The twins returned with a sterling silver tray, a full bottle of Blanton's Bourbon riding majestically atop, framed by two pewter goblets. The goblets were ice cold, condensation trickling down the sides. The girls set the tray down and attempted to pour, but Cannery gave a dismissive wave and they scurried away. She poured both goblets about three quarters full.

"Why dangerous?" I asked.

"There's a new element in Cable, people we could do without. They've come to think of The Site as their home away from home, wherever the hell that might be. I think they come here to recruit local boys into their group."

"I don't want any trouble for you," I said with genuine concern.

She looked at me with a little hurt in her eyes, "Nobody's going to bring any harm on Cannery Row. Besides love, I believe in looking after people I care about."

"So, what have you heard?"

"There's a bad moon rising, I can tell you that for sure."

Chapter 17

Cannery explained that one of her girls overheard some of the new guys talking about livestock. She said they never actually *said* someone had killed anything, but it was obvious these fellows had already done something—and were planning something much bigger. I asked which girl, and Cannery pointed to a trim black woman dancing on the scaffolding.

"What's her name?"

Cannery smiled, looked me in the eye so she could measure my response and said, "Back Hoe."

"Ah, Cannery, you do have a way with the names. What might a more civilized sort of gentleman call her?"

She faked a half pissed off and half-pout look. I smiled without showing teeth. It's the look I use when attempting charm. It worked. Cannery grinned, took a pen clipped to the button rig of my shirt, and wrote on a bar napkin shaped like a dump truck. She put the pen back saying, "Cloud, this is a Friday night, and these ladies are *working*. I wouldn't let anyone else in the world near them if it weren't about paying business. And I don't want trouble for any of my girls, so why don't you give her a call at this number tomorrow? Tell her I said it was all right for her to talk to you."

"I appreciate this. What's your take on the guys she was talking about?"

"They've been coming in for about a year, maybe a little more. They always go into the back and shoot pool. They don't associate with any of the locals for the most part, but every once in a while they bring in some farm boy or would-be ranch hand and get them all liquored up and pay for one of the girls to service the new recruit. They never partake of the girls themselves. They always pay up and don't ever get into any scuffles. That's a might different than the regular crowd, kind of sets them apart."

She suddenly tilted her head, looking over my shoulder. She seemed a little startled, which was odd for her. She had seen it all, and in my time knowing her, she had never flinched at anything. I started to turn around, and she reached out to squeeze my hand, stopping me.

"What's going on here? You look spooked, and I've never seen you spooked," I said.

"Sweet Love, there is more to the story, but I just can't get into it right now. You best be finishing your drink and heading out."

With that, she got up, obviously shaken, and grabbed the tray of bourbon. She made an exhibition of visiting the next table and offering a shot of the bottle as if it were a normal custom. I casually looked around for anyone who didn't seem to belong. *He* was tall and very lean, like a snake surveying his territory. He was wearing all black except for a glint of a silver bracelet, like John Wayne wore at the end. He wore wire-rimmed shades despite the dank fog of the bar room. A strange mood took over the place. The dancers worked harder. The bartenders and waitress hustled a little more. What the hell was going on here? Who was this stranger? He looked fake, but everyone in the bar oozed fear.

When in doubt, shake things up.

I got up and walked toward the dark stranger. He made a point of not seeing me approach. When I got within a couple of steps, two other men I hadn't seen moved closer and flanked him. I put out my hand to greet him and he faced me for the first time, but he ignored my hand and made a point of keeping his own at his side, the silver bracelet glimmering. Then he slowly turned and the three of them slipped through a green door next to the bar. Plainly, I wasn't welcome to follow.

The bar room took an almost audible sigh and things returned to normal.

I left the bar. There was definitely something going on. But I really didn't want to make trouble for Cannery or any of the women working there. I'd be back, and next time I would bring friends.

Since I didn't make any on this visit.

***

On my way home I began to put together a schedule for the next day. It would be Saturday, but that didn't matter much dealing with people in Cable. Saturday was a workday—the cows and other livestock didn't know the difference. They expected to be tended to even on the weekends, inconsiderate bastards that they were. Dairy farmers even had to work Sundays. Many of the sanctified looked down their collective noses at this practice, but again, the cows didn't know the difference, and so the people who milked them worked the cows' schedule.

I usually have pretty short mornings, preferring to start around ten. The work I do has many possibilities during the evening hours, so it fits rather nicely. I have a recorder built into the cab of my truck that works on voice recognition. I use it to assemble notes and to make a calendar when I'm really feeling organized.

I spoke the password, bringing the recorder on line, then made some notes about the case. I gave the calendar command and told the recorder tomorrow morning I would visit another of the ranchers who'd lost a bull.

The home front was dark and quiet. I showered and went to bed. Tomorrow was brimming with possibilities. I slept soundly, despite the possibilities.

Chapter 18

Bent Daleen — Deep in the Scrub

Bent Daleen held a meeting. He'd been busy for years setting his plan in motion. He now commanded the services of a small army, about a hundred people in all, pulled together out of a population short on education and money. The army was his buffer, and he considered all of his charges expendable in the pursuit of his cause.

Phase one of the plan had required patience, planning, the poisoning. Now things would move more rapidly. Daleen, the Prophet, chose this particular rural location for a simple reason: he figured news, other than town gossip, would travel a little slower. This would give him the delays he needed once the action began in earnest.

Everything had gone better than he'd planned. The locals were stumped as to the origin of the crimes committed and hadn't summoned any high-powered help. Their best efforts were in the hands of a local, private law man who was well known but not everyone's favorite person. Still, this imp had started poking around into things which could derail Daleen's plans and something had to be done.

That was what the meeting was about.

The investigator had to go. Daleen was a severe man who didn't miss details. Better to make it look like a traffic accident or something benign. Nonetheless, it had to be done somewhere that wouldn't bring suspicion anywhere near the compound.

He decided to assemble a ten-man crew and outline the plan for taking the investigator out. The prime directive was this couldn't be an *attempt*. At all costs the mission must succeed.

He placed a black leather bag on the table. It contained an arsenal, which should make the job easy, if it became necessary. The Prophet handed out three vehicle keys and gave explicit instructions. Only use the guns if the mission is going to fail. The first choice is the accident scenario, run the man off the road and make sure his neck is broken in the crash. If not in the crash, then someone must do it personally. Take him out alone, no witnesses. He adjourned the meeting with military efficiency.

Then Daleen got back to the business of outlining the assault of Phase Two.

Chapter 19

Emma and Blue were early risers, even on Saturdays. Even on their birthdays, even... well you get my drift. They always got up early. In the beginning stages of our relationship, it bothered me, but now I just stretched out and enjoyed the cool vacant sheets enveloping our bed. At around eight-thirty, a nagging beam of sunlight pierced between the curtains and I couldn't sleep any more, even though I really wanted to.

I rose and scratched, long and complete. I sleep in a pair of gray athletic shorts—it makes the task of changing into something comfortable for the morning settled. I grabbed a jug of Gatorade from the fridge and went to the front deck of the house. The ladies were gardening. The front of our house is a virtual jungle. Every plant loves our climate and Emma and Blue see fit to give each and every one a permanent place to live.

The way Emma and Blue garden is not made up of frilly white dresses and greenhouses. They get dirty. It's like they're fighting a war against weeds, soil, and the plants they love. I become more smitten each time I watch them soaking in sweat with dirt stains on their faces.

I picked up a beach chair and a book of mystery short stories. If conversation could be kept to an absolute minimum, it looked to be an absolutely perfect start to the day.

The ladies finally noticed me and waved. I waved back and began reading. No matter how good the story, I always get distracted when they're working the garden. To me there is nothing sexier than passionate women really getting after it. They were talking to each other pretty much the entire time, yet I couldn't pick up a single word or sentence. That's probably the way it should be.

After an hour they came to where I was sitting in the shade and sat down on the ground. Blue drained about half the remaining Gatorade then passed it to Emma, who finished it off. Blue wore a handkerchief tying her hair back, exposing her beautiful freckled face to more of the rich sunlight which made them grow in size and number. Emma wore a large, floppy, straw hat with a long flowing ribbon.

We all looked contently over the gardening. I really could tell no difference, but that would remain a guarded secret. Blue spoke up, "What's on the day's agenda for the super sleuth?"

"I have to run over to Dan Hall's ranch in the corner of Marion County this morning."

"Oh good, we can ride over to the ranch with you and visit the flea market, while you search for dark secrets," Emma said.

"What in the world could you possibly need from the flea market?"

They looked at each other as if it were obvious. "Tomato plants, of course. I told you the other day we needed a dozen or so to complete the *red* part of the garden." Blue said contemptuously.

"The market is three or four miles from the ranch."

"No matter. We'll take our bikes and you can come pick us up when you're done," Emma said.

I do love to go for a ride with this beautiful twosome. A family outing was under way.

***

Forty-five minutes later I was sitting in the truck with Jake and Jack, enjoying Hank Williams Jr. tell us country boys can survive. The dogs intermittently wrestled then stared into the air conditioning vents. If only all of life's pleasures were so simple.

The ladies rounded the back porch, bicycles in tow. They were a vision, wearing white sundresses and wide-brimmed straw hats. The bikes each sported a large basket filled with fresh flowers. I told the boys to stay and went to help load the bikes. "What are the flowers for?"

"To sell at the market. If we do it just right, we can make enough money to cover the cost of the tomatoes," Blue said.

In the truck, Blue ejected the perfectly good Hank Williams Jr. disk and produced another from a local band I was familiar with, but not as intimately as the women. Sister Hazel. I was pleased but pouted all the same so they would know *I* was still the king of *at least* my office/truck. The conversation was continuous, and I was not asked very often for my opinion.

About five miles out on the old country road between Alachua and Marion Counties, I noticed a squat, gray-green vehicle in the rear view mirror. It was gaining on us quickly. I was casual about it until the vehicle started tailgating on a road where passing was easy and I was only going sixty or so. Then another identical vehicle appeared behind the first, obviously in tandem with the first.

I interrupted the conversation to tell the ladies to tighten their buckles. Blue, now alert to the threat, picked up my gaze in the rear view mirror. "What's up, Babe?"

"We've got friends," I said, reaching behind the seat for the .357 Colt Python I use to scare the crap out of anyone who sees it. I tried a playful tone. "Emma, have you made some enemies in the English department?"

Emma wasn't accustomed to violence, except vicariously through Blue and me. She looked at us for reassurance and saw the steel in both of our eyes. She settled back in the seat like a scared but confident kid getting ready for her first ride on a wild rollercoaster.

Blue shifted from the middle to the door seat of the truck. Emma was now book ended by trust. I handed Blue the big pistol, she checked the cylinder and gave the password to the mobile phone unit. She was all business now.

"Call 555-5959," she said with grit. The floral print straw hat was in the floorboard.

A voice echoed from the speakerphone. "Dispatch."

A flurry of codes and numbers ensued. "Agent six-one-eight, I am 1010 (off duty), and being pursued, need immediate code 20 (assistance) on State

Road 219, about eight miles inside Alachua County. Notify Marion County deputies we are crossing county line in approximately three minutes. Be advised, two vehicles, both Army Surplus Hummers, are attempting 1156 (vehicular assault). I am currently passenger in new model, black, RAM 2500 four-by-four and will be taking evasive action." She shut the phone down.

I looked over at Blue. "Evasive action?"

"That's what it needs to say on the tape. Get the speed up as fast as you can handle."

I was momentarily plagued by ego. "As fast as *I* can handle?"

"Cut the shit, Cloud, and do exactly what I tell you. Put the hammer down and run from this fight if you can." She crawled into the rear of the king cab and slid open a window.

I didn't *want* to run from this fight. Not only for the usual caveman reasons, but because I wanted to know who was in the other vehicles and who sent them. All that being said, Blue was right—we had Emma and the dogs with us, and I'm sure we were outnumbered. I would try to make a run for it, but the big diesel engine was built for power, not speed.

The two Hummers began swerving from lane to lane. "They're going to try and pass you, don't let them," Blue calmly said.

Don't let them. I realized my truck was going to be, in all likelihood, seriously damaged. I once saw Wyatt Earp slap a man with a rope for hitting his horse. I felt this was the correct response.

I did a pretty good job of blocking the vehicles from passing until we crossed the county line and the road turned to crap. There were giant potholes and cracks in the Marion County side of 219. I was keeping the speed up around a hundred miles an hour and a pothole at that speed would be an ugly situation. A log truck bloomed on the horizon coming our way in the other lane. The weaving and maneuvering became more rapid and frantic. Just as the log truck topped the hill in front of us, the other vehicles fell in behind me again.

We passed the log truck, but on the other side of the hill sat another Hummer, in our lane and already up to speed. They were going to try and box us in. Blue got back on the mobile phone.

"Dispatch."

"Agent six-one-eight. Where the hell is my code 20, dispatch?"

"Be advised six-one-eight, two Marion deputies are enroute. What is your 1020?"

"One mile over the county line. When can I expect contact?"

"It will still be five minutes or so—they had a long way to come."

"In five minutes, this'll all be over, one way or the other. Tell them to get here *now* and that we've picked up a third Hummer. Out."

Sometimes Blue is displeased with the initiative and hustle her fellow officers demonstrate. "Sorry bastards were sitting on their asses somewhere. Took them five minutes to finish their donuts and now that same five minutes is going to be *our* ass."

I pulled a second .357 Python from my shoulder holster and laid it across my lap. Emma glanced at it and turned back at the road. She didn't approve of any of this. Even if it wasn't my fault, I was almost as bad as the guys in the Hummers. Jake and Jack were moving from window to window letting out growls which could strike fear into the heart of any hamster hearing them.

"Blue, they're getting ready to try and box us in. This guy up front is already slowing down," I said.

"I know; I know. Jesus Christ, where the hell are those deputies?"

"We're going to have to do this a little outside the book. We can't get boxed in or we're fish in a barrel, if they start shooting—which I figure will be in about forty seconds when we get to the Old Oak Bridge."

Blue breathed heavy, she didn't like doing anything in her job outside the book. I was surprised when Emma said, "He's right, let's get them before they get us."

"All right, what should we do?"

"When we get about fifty yards from the bridge I want you to shoot out the front tires of the Hummer behind us. I'm going to ram the back end of the one in front and see if he drives or swims better. That'll hopefully leave just one, then I'll pull over on the side of the road and if they do the same, we're going to beat the living shit out of them. What do you think?"

"It'll work if we can use the bridge as a pick."

Emma slid over next to the door, grabbed Jack and held him in her lap as the dog growled and pushed his wet nose against the window. "I like the beat the shit out of them part," she muttered.

Both Blue and I looked at her, then at each other. This could work.

The bridge was only a hundred yards in front of us and closing fast.

"Get ready and make the shots count."

Blue swung the barrel of the Python through the window.

I measured the situation one last time and decided it was go time. I put my game face on and jammed the accelerator to the floor. The truck didn't exactly spring into action, but it pulled ahead with all cylinders pumping. "Alright Blue, now," I said with forced calm.

Simultaneously, we rammed the back of the Hummer in front of us and Blue began firing at the tires of the vehicle behind. An arm appeared from the closest Hummer, holding a large handgun. Two distinct shots.

The cab of the truck was assaulted with ear pounding sound — the screech of the tires, the impact of the bumpers, and the deafening boom of the pistol. Jake jumped into the floorboard of the passenger's side. Emma screamed and both Blue and I looked over to see a spray of blood on her chest and Jack lying in her lap.

Our pursuers realized too late they were now on defense rather than offense. We could make out at least three heads in the vehicle in front of us thrashing about in a cloud of upturned arms and hands, as if swatting a swarm of killer bees. The vehicle behind slammed on the brakes. The momentum carried them forward, first straight then sideways. They slammed into the railing of the bridge and launched into the air on a slow spiral, Dukes of Hazzard style. For a moment they seemed to fly over us, then dropped out of sight heading for the river below.

The Hummer in front fishtailed and almost got a good grip again before launching over the opposite side of the bridge. We drove through the tire smoke and confusion like a NASCAR driver blasting through a multi-car wreck on a high bank turn.

I hit the brakes and the tires locked, throwing us against the seat belts until we slid to a halt. Panicked, I placed a hand on Emma's bloody chest. I couldn't tell if she was hit bad or not—she looked to be in shock one way or the other. In the rear view mirror I saw the remaining Hummer still sitting on the opposite side of the bridge. The driver was weighing the possibilities of coming after us on his own.

Better to be the lion than the gazelle. I shoved the diesel into reverse and floored it again, sending smoke burning black from the tires. Blue leveled the pistol and prepared to fire again.

Speechless, Emma grabbed my arm, her eyes locked ahead. The deputies were coming over the hill. Emma wanted me to stop and let the cavalry lay down some heavy fire. I would have kept going, except Emma is the mature one, never over-dramatizing a situation, she's the mothering sort.

And she's always right.

I braked hard again. The Hummer on the other side made an abrupt U-turn and sped off in the opposite direction. Two Marion County deputy cars screeched to a halt in front of my truck, and with that, the adrenaline pump seethed but had no release. We all sat in the truck, breathing hard, sweating like crowded hogs and ready to be all too hostile to the ones we loved.

Blue saw the large bloody spray on Emma's chest. She came over the back seat and put her hands on either side of Emma's face. "Emma, Emma, are you all right?" Emma's eyes bulged with fear and shock. I leaned over and ripped her blouse open, rubbing my hand over her chest, smearing the blood as I tried in vain to find an entry wound. I jumped from the cab and ran around to her side, snatching the door open. My legs buckled at the sight. Both women were attempting to stop a pulsing flow of blood from Jack's chest. The little dog was shaking uncontrollably, his white and beige fur soaked in deep black blood. He looked with huge brown eyes at each one of us. The question was there behind the pain and fear. *What happened? How could you let me hurt this bad?*

I reached in and felt the bloody chest of the little dog. There was an enormous hole just below his breastbone. He convulsed, then with one last shudder went still. His tongue lolled to the side of his mouth and a trickle of blood dripped from its pink tip.

I slid my hands under his body and took him from Emma's lap. She and

Blue fell from the cab and all three of us knelt on the hot pavement, looking at the bloody carcass in my hands.

Jake jumped to the ground and came to his best friend's side. He sniffed with vigor and attempted to nuzzle the limp body to life. He whimpered and then looked at me. I was frozen.

Blue grabbed Jake and hugged him ferociously. Both women began to wail in angry, sad sobs.

***

The Marion County deputies swarmed over the truck, checking us out and making sure we were all right. They were plainly feeling the guilt of letting a fellow law enforcer down.

Blue barked at them, "Get the hell away from us, take your sorry slow asses down to the river, and see if anyone is still alive." She said this without a speck of pity—she only wanted to ask any survivors questions.

The deputies blocked off the bridge, and within minutes, seven more cars arrived on the scene, one driven by the Marion County Sheriff himself, Oren Block.

***

For an hour, the Marion Sheriff and his deputies questioned us about the events leading up to the wreck. Although they were professional, there didn't seem to be much concern for us, and certainly not for our little dead dog. This made Blue more than pissed. She did most of the talking and she reached her threshold when Sheriff Block prodded her about why someone would try and run us off the road. She turned her head toward the ground, then skyward, and breathed a long sigh.

Hurricane Blue was getting ready to unleash her fury; I was glad I would not be in its path.

Just at that moment, MacGregor Knox arrived, calmly joining us where we were looking over the dead remains of Jack on the tailgate of my truck. Block saw him first and bristled like a rooster getting ready for the fight of his life. Knox took off his Stetson and made a wide gesture of confliction as he wiped his forehead with a red handkerchief. He touched Blue's shoulder, saying something we couldn't hear.

She said, "Cloud, could you help me get Jack and Emma back in the truck?"

I was the pawn, struck by the severity, yet calm in the moment. I did as I was asked. Blue carefully placed Jack in the basket which only an hour and a half ago held flowers from our yard. Then she whispered in Emma's ear.

Emma got back into the cab of the truck, a blank look on her face. Blue set the basket in her lap. She didn't respond, letting the basket sit there, her hands on her bloody knees with palms up.

Sheriff Oren Block looked as if he wanted to protest the removal of an eyewitness. Knox looked at him with a contempt and rage that said, *Say one word to her, and I'll shoot you where you stand.*

Knox said to me, "Why don't you walk with Blue down to the river and see what you can find out?"

It wasn't a request. I looked deep into my friend's granite eyes and knew he would extract a pound of ass-meat from his fellow law officer. I would only complicate things by sticking around. And Blue would positively cause a scene.

"Come on, Blue, let's walk down to the river."

She looked at Knox and he nodded. We headed off through the thick grass down toward the water. As we left I heard Knox speak through clenched teeth to Sheriff Block.

"I was wondering if I might have a word with you, Oren?"

***

Below the bridge and out of sight, we lingered and listened in. My friend Knox is not an agitated man. He always seemed a little too docile to me to be an aggressive law enforcer. But I could hear he wasn't the anything like that now.

Block began, "Mac, I don't know what the hell you think you're doing. This is Marion County, and I'm conducting an investigation into a major crime. You can't just ride up on your white horse and release a material witness without my consent."

"Shut the fuck up, Oren. You were trying to question one of my agents, a Cable Counties Agent, about an incident originating in the Cable Counties. You were acting as if she's a criminal. You're ass-covering because your donut-eaters were late on the response to an officer under duress. The only reason you're still in the standing position is because she wasn't hurt. 'Cause I tell ya, Oren, if she or the other one had more than a few hairs out of place, I would stomp a mud hole in that fat carcass of yours. You understand where I'm coming from?"

"Mac, you can't threaten me."

"Oren, you were *just barely* good enough to be elected last time. I don't get elected. I'm appointed by the Governor himself, as you well know. If you fuck with me on this or on the ensuing investigation, I'll make sure you aren't good enough to make sheriff again. Furthermore, you will make a complete investigation of this crime scene and you will send a copy of it to me at my office *before* you file it with the state. If I feel the need to correct your grammar or add some punctuation or anything else, you will make those corrections. *Now*, do you see where I'm coming from?"

Sheriff Oren Block was stymied, his shoulders hunching. He knew his limitations and wanted no part of a competent, tough man like Knox. Block removed his hat and wiped his sleeve across his face. He then walked back toward the other side of the bridge, his shoulders a little hunched, his step a little slow.

Chapter 20

The Scrub

The three men in the remaining Hummer rode in silence for a good piece. Each in their own way pondered the consequences awaiting when they returned and admitted their failure to the Prophet, Daleen. One of the men, who wore a bright green John Deere hat spoke first, "I say we just keep driving, head over to the Gulf and see if we can sell this big-assed piece of crap, take the money, split it up, and go our separate ways." Another, a local recruit and the brother of John Deere cap, his face contorted in fear and disbelief said, "Yeah, I'm not of a mind to tell the Prophet about our fuck-up and see what punishment he lays on us."

The driver had come to the cause early on. He sat in silence, listening to the simpering whelps scared for their own skin, speaking of desertion. *He would stand before the Prophet and tell the tale of failure, never considering running away. He expected punishment. All armies had to maintain discipline.*

He swerved onto a dirt-graded road leading to the compound, his actions doing the talking.

***

The three men from the Hummer stood in a bleak cinder-block room. The two local recruits were a step behind the driver and examining the floor for cracks. John Deere cap wrung the hat in his hands. His brother tried hard not to show his fear, but still trembled.

Behind a large wooden table, the Prophet, Daleen, sat looking steely and cold at them. He took in the whole story as the driver related their failure to carry out the mission. Long ago, Daleen learned to hide his rage. It always bubbled below the surface like hot sulfuric mud, but he trained himself to put his mind in another place when the demons were itching to boil out onto the people around him. A strong leader was allowed his rage but could only show it in a controlled way. He could exact punishment and even torture, but must always remain in control of his emotions or other followers might think him shallow and common.

When the driver fell silent, The Prophet put his hands to his face and sat still, breathing the dank aroma of palm sweat. The three men wanted to apologize. They wanted to throw themselves at his feet and beg forgiveness—yet they'd learned from Daleen that weakness was worse than failure. They stood agonizing over the inevitable punishment.

After a long silence, Daleen stood and walked to the block wall. With his finger, he trailed the grout in the seam across to the heavy oak door, the only one in the room. The three men watched in horror as Daleen shut the door and locked it tight with a chain and padlock.

Daleen returned to the table, leaning forward, his hands resting on the surface, his shoulders bunched and a tension building in his forearms as he looked into the eyes of each man.

Finally, he spoke. "You have failed the cause. You have failed your brothers and sisters who have worked so long and hard to see our dream through to reality. You have failed me and therefore have failed God. Only one of us will leave this room alive."

Chapter 21

Back at the Old Oak Bridge

The recovery of the waterlogged vehicles ground on. They probably wouldn't have the wrecked Hummers out of the water until sometime around midnight. Two bodies had been recovered from each vehicle, but one man had been thrown free and was in critical condition. He'd been transported by ambulance to the University Teaching Hospital on the same campus where Emma worked.

Knox walked over to the bank of the river where Blue and I were watching the recovery efforts. "Blue, I want you and Cloud to take Emma home. I'll call you later and tell you if we've found anything."

Blue never questions the orders of her boss, but she didn't want to leave the crime scene. "I'd like to stay on, if it's all the same to you."

"No, Blue. It isn't all the same to me. I want you to get out of here and take care of your family. That's an order."

***

We were back on the road driving home. Blue was in a bad mood, and it wasn't because we'd almost been killed—and it was only in part because our family had been subtracted by one. Emma stared straight ahead, the basket still in her lap. I could hardly move an eyelash for the thickness of tension and sorrow in the cab. I knew my job was to drive and keep my mouth shut.

After about five minutes of silence, Blue spoke up. "He still treats me like I was his *daughter*, not one of his agents. If it had been one of the male agents, he wouldn't have sent *them* home."

Ever the problem solver, I was busting at the seams to tell Blue what I thought about Knox's sympathetic gesture, even calling us a family. But I resisted and just grabbed the steering wheel tighter. Blue was parlaying her sorrow into anger. She does that. Emma said nothing.

"I mean—what the hell? How am I ever going to prove my abilities if the AIC is always protecting me? Mac's your friend, but he's my boss. I'm damn sick and tired of him *handling* me."

What was unspoken was that Blue had for some time had her eye on a Federal badge. She'd taken the job with the Cable Department of Law Enforcement to gain some experience. She always planned on going on to the FBI. Our little "family" stalled her plans, and for quite some time the subject of her pursuing a career on a Federal level had gone away. Emma and I knew if Blue were to pursue the FBI avenue, she would surely have to move to one of the big cities. There just wasn't enough of the kind of crime requiring Federal attention in the Cable Counties.

"He should put me in charge of the investigation. I'm the one with first-hand knowledge of the suspects. Who else is going to go balls-out to solve this thing, Charley Smith, Jim Turner? I don't think so. He treats me like a little girl who's too fragile."

She was hurting and I tried to let her rant.

"I'm a department decoration, not a capable agent. It's all well and good when I'm competing in the state police Olympics, bringing home the gold for the small-time country department, but when it comes to real police work, I'm just a kid."

My heart knew to keep my mouth shut. My brain was saying, *Solve the problem dummy*. It was a simple tic-tac-toe board and my impulses were screaming, *Put the X in the middle, dumb ass*.

I strained, I tried hard, I swear. My brain won out. I started tentatively, "Blue...."

She was emotionally cornered, and I knew it. She was waiting for something, an explanation, another point of view, but in one word I unintentionally intoned pity. This was the worst, totally unacceptable.

She wasn't frantic and didn't want any comforting. She'd been almost baiting me to say something and when I did her words came across the cab of the truck calm, but with a jagged edged.

"You know you're not supposed to say anything. You're just supposed to *listen*. You know this and still you let that mouth of yours begin to flap."

I wanted to retrofire the rockets. I wanted to hurt her in that moment with words, which would make her feel the same way she just made *me* feel. Fortunately, the sight of Emma made me hold my tongue. I bit the inside of my mouth and stayed silent.

Chapter 22

It began to rain on the way home. It was the perfect setting for the mood we were all in. I got out in the downpour to open the gate. When I returned to the cab, the women had emotionally changed places. Blue was sobbing uncontrollably and Emma held her in a tight embrace.

The tires crunched through the wet mulched driveway. I pulled the truck directly in front of the house, driving over a small stand of ferns the women had planted. No one noticed.

The latch of the truck door seemed heavy, as did the whole situation. I went around to the passenger's side. Emma released Blue and handed me the basket with our beloved buddy. I set it on the toolbox and noticed rain drops began to cascade over the crimson tattoo of blood on Jack's fur.

The women and Jake tumbled from the cab, and Emma reached for the basket. I grabbed her wrist. "Don't," I said. "Just take Blue inside and I'll take care of Jack."

She slowly withdrew her arm, her eyes filling again with tears at the mention of his name. She helped Blue across the drive—the normally towering presence of personality that was Blue, shaded by the physically superior form of Emma. They hugged each other as they walked up the railroad tie steps. Jake stayed behind with me and his pal.

I went behind the house to the wooden barn and pulled on the stubborn door. In exasperation, I cursed and pulled again. The door held firm. Rain soaked me straight through. Without thinking, I took a step back and kicked violently at the sodden wood. The door gave a little and I followed with a face-first entry. I felt the splintered wood rake against my cheeks and liked the feeling of pain. I wanted to feel mean.

I searched the dark spider-webbed interior for tools. Standing in the corner was a set of posthole diggers. With an angry swipe I used them as a battering ram to break back through the shattered doors.

I threw the diggers in the back of the truck, set the basket reverently on the passenger seat and let Jake leap into the cab. I slammed the door as if it were the enemy.

Near the swamp end of the property, I began to dig with an immense hatred for the earth. On my knees, I buried the tool as hard as I could into the sodden earth. When I hit something hard, I tossed the hole-diggers aside and scraped with my hands. Jake dug furiously beside me. I was vaguely aware of the blood dripping from my fingers as I flung earth in all directions. When a deafening clack of thunder followed a brilliant streak of lightning, I saw I had made an enormous hole, enough for burying a person, not a dog.

I took the basket from the passenger seat, lifted Jack out, and held the dog in my arms awhile.

Jake and Jack had been my one-year anniversary present to Emma and Blue, given on Christmas day. Two puppies, just balls of fur really, tumbling from a wrapped basket much like the one I just used to bring Jack here. The ladies were elated I'd succumbed to letting pets of any kind come to live with us.

In the time I'd known him, Jack was the most full-of-life soul I ever encountered. He was my buddy, the one who always took my side in an argument. He was the one who lay at my feet when I worked at the computer and guarded the door of the bathroom when I did my business. He was the closest thing I could imagine to a son, and he was my friend.

I gently lay Jack in the dark cavernous clutch of mother earth. I wanted to apologize for having put him in harms' way, but he wouldn't have wanted an apology.

I filled the hole until I was at a loss for loose earth, then I clawed at the sides of the grave with my hands again.

With the mound reflecting a monument of ashes to ashes and dust to dust, I laid a large white limestone rock on top. There were no words left, and no emotion. Jake and I left the truck where it was and walked through the storm back to the house of sorrow.

Chapter 23

Bent Daleen sat in as close to despair as he would let himself recognize. Going after the PI was a gamble. If it had succeeded, then Phase Two could ease on without interruption. But, the gamble went bad and now there would be more attention—perhaps Federal attention. He cursed the scraps of human waste he'd sent on such a seemingly simple mission.

Now he would need to accelerate the pace. Phase Two was to be filled with shock and awe.

Chapter 24

Cloud, Emma & Blue

Sundays for us was traditionally a day to pursue our own little interests, a day to be by ourselves until the evening when we generally got together for dinner. But this wasn't a traditional Sunday. This was the day after. Our family had been lessened by one, and we were all feeling it. I needed to clear my head of emotions.

I got up and went for a run around the property. If I stay to the fence line, it comes out to about five miles. I made it about half way before I petered out. Even though my previous life with the government was physically demanding and I'd retained much of my fitness, I just didn't feel like making the effort. In the past, I'd seen and even caused a lot of death. Now the reaper had visited my own home. Instead of running, I walked the entire loop again thinking over the case and about life without Jack.

In every crime, it's always a good rule of thumb to follow the money. I thought about the possibility of profit as a motive for killing the bulls. There were a few, but they seemed light, not the kind that lead to killing people. So, I figured it had to be drugs. The connection between this outside dark force and the chilly response I got from Cannery Row all pointed in that direction. My working theory was that somebody was moving drugs in Cable and trying to divert attention by killing off prized livestock. Thin, I know, but sometimes you have to get positively anorexic to get the truth.

Another bothersome thought was the bulls had all been killed in secluded areas. Knox and I hadn't caught much gossip as a result. It's usually just a matter of time before someone talks to a friend who embellishes and passes on the gossip and before you know it, the information finds its way to someone with a conscience.

So far, the only people who seemed to know anything were the Gallagher boys and Cannery Row. When the dark man came in the bar, she'd closed up—we'd never had that kind of relationship. I had to go back and find out what was left unsaid.

I also needed to check with Knox and find out if they'd been able to lift any evidence from the crashed Hummers. And what about that? Military Hummers, three of them? That was a lot more organized than most of our local country-boy hoodlums could conjure up.

I made the turn toward home and decided to cut across the edge of a small swamp bordering the western boundary of the property.

As I walked out the far end of the swamp, I saw maybe fifteen people on the edge of the pasture. They were all dressed in shorts and several of the men were shirtless. Thinking I'd accidentally come upon the very people I was hunting, I crouched behind a large pine tree and watched. It was the middle of the day, which wasn't in keeping with when the bulls were killed, and the lone bull I have on property was far from a prize. I had recently thought about looking into the bovine equivalent of Viagra.

Still, these were trespassers, and a county road was just a hop, step and a jump across a neighbor's pasture. I watched for a good ten minutes as the group wandered around, searching the ground. After a moment it occurred to me, these were 'shroomers. College kids from the local University who, on occasion, trekked out into the manure filled pastures to hunt for mushrooms.

I would have let them alone had it not been so close to the house. If they wanted to fuzz out a few brain cells sampling the native fungus, what the hell. But they were too close to the house, and I wasn't comfortable with the thought of some kid hopped up on hallucinogenic mushrooms wandering up to the house one day when I wasn't there asking Blue, or worse, Emma, to use the john.

I figured they'd been doing some sampling as they picked, so I was pretty sure I could out run them to the fence bordering the property. I came from behind the pine and started a slow trot towards where I thought they would try and jump the fence. I got to within about a hundred yards before any of them noticed me, then they freaked and started stumbling toward the fence. It was every man and women for themselves. They dropped bags and pieces of clothing, and a few even ran right out of their shoes. One poor kid, who must have been sampling more than picking, couldn't decide which way to go and just kind of ran in a big circle. I broke into a sprint and easily cut them off, reaching the fence before any of them. The first one who got close decided to try a little razzle-dazzle move and go around me. Harkening back to my football days, I made short work of his hip wiggle and buried him with a head-first tackle. I jumped up and pulled another guy off the fence. He was struggling with the top strand of barbed wire. Another stringy kid ran right into a fence post and fell backward as if flattened in a cartoon. The rest of the pack stopped in their tracks, defeat on their shiny, sweat-covered faces. I simply pointed toward an oak tree standing within the fence line and the small band of fungus-eaters slunk reluctantly toward its inviting shade.

I went over to the kid who got intimate with the fence post. He was out cold. I threw him over my shoulder and gave a hand up to the first boy I tackled. He was covered in cow shit, blubbering and crying. I set the post tackler down in the shade and two of the girls wiped his forehead with wet bandanas.

For the next few minutes we all sat there, silent. I was letting let the effects of the mushrooms fade, before I gave them the sermon. After a bit I stood up and began lecturing them on the terrible effects of eating mushrooms, and that I was of a mind to call the local Sheriff and have them arrested for trespassing. All seemed sufficiently paranoid of the law except for one kid in a bright orange football jersey. He stood stupidly right in front of me. I hadn't considered the fact they might fight back. My odds weren't good, even in their altered state.

He looked at me, eyes glazed over, and started to grin. He wasn't *trying* me; he just couldn't help seeing the humor in everything.

"Heeey maaan, aren't you that guy, the one…the one…?"

I nodded.

"Man, we aren't hurting anybody, and besides if you let us go, I got some good info for you."

I wasn't impressed. What could this kid possibly know that would interest me?

"Man, I heard you were after the guys who've been killing all of the bulls around here. Guess what? I know who they are."

Okay, now I *was* impressed—maybe. I leaned in close, getting a bad whiff of stale dog breath. "Well, well, young master 'shroom-head might just know the magic words. Whatcha got?"

"It's the Seekers, man. They the one's terrorizing the countryside."

"Who're the Seekers?"

"Aw man, you don't know shit if you don't know about the Seekers. They're the dark side of the force man, the black man in the moon, the Anti-Christ resurrected."

"Names, dead-head. What are their names?"

"C'mon man, I don't know names. They're like the black fog at night. They just sweep in and do their evil deeds."

This boy was a little too poetic in his current mind set. He'd given me a lead, but he wouldn't be any further help now. I wheeled him around and grabbed his wallet from his back pocket. He thrashed a little, lost his balance, and fell down. I found a student card from the university and a driver's license. I took out the license and threw the wallet back at him.

I bent down to eye level. "Now I know who you are, Brantley Snow, and real soon I'm going to come and have a talk with you. You'll remember my hospitality when I come, and I hope you *do* have some information I can appreciate." I straightened up. "Now all of you get off of my land and don't ever come back or I'll turn my dogs loose on you. They are big, mean, and make Cujo look like a kitty. Now git!" Before it was out of my mouth I realized I said "dogs." There weren't *dogs* left, there was just Jake.

The kids' exodus over the fence was a short film on the evils of drugs. I would have laid down laughing, if I hadn't wanted to seem so mean and intimidating—and if I weren't mourning my little buddy.

Chapter 25

Back at the house the ladies were again furiously working the garden. They saw me coming and met me at the gate. Blue leaned seductively against the galvanized steel. She dramatized a battery of eyelid maneuvers, which always makes my legs a little weak. They were trying to move on, to replace the loss and pain.

"Emma and I want to go for a ride in the plane."

"What do I get if I take you for this ride?"

Emma gave a sultry sigh. "A sandwich."

I had been thinking of something else, but I was hungry. "Maybe a nice turkey and Swiss with all the trimmings?"

They looked at each other and positively giggled. Blue said, "You can have one of those too, but that's not the kind of sandwich we were thinking of."

I have heard that many people try to bury their sorrow after a funeral by coupling.

Well, tally-ho, onward and upward, I thought with a devilish smile.

***

I didn't keep the plane at any airport. I bought the property because it had its own landing strip near the back in a separate fenced area. Emma and Blue made a picnic basket with snacks, and I brought my map of locations where the bulls were killed figuring I could fly over the areas I'd marked and the ladies wouldn't know I was working, instead of just passing time on the wing.

The Beechcraft lifted from the runway like a familiar smooth song, and we were up, up and away. I circled our property and the ladies were quickly engrossed, pointing out new developments made in the garden since our last flight.

I'm not sure what I expected to find. Sometimes it just seemed the smart thing to do was to look at everything from every angle and that includes the air for me. It's amazing the things you run into or turn over by accident just sorting through facts and locations.

The Beechcraft came with navigational equipment allowing you to program locations, and the plane will fly there on cruise control. I consulted my notes and loaded in the five locations where the bull kills happened, as well as where the first woman was murdered. I called air traffic control and got permission to keep the plane at a relatively low altitude.

Flying over the counties, I always remembered why I chose to come back here. It's absolutely beautiful. The rural landscape was woven together into a bright quilt of different shades of green and punctuated by hundreds of small ponds and larger lakes. Timber companies long ago discovered the climate was as good as any to grow pine trees for pulpwood. There were tens of thousands of acres of timber within the Cable Counties. This, along with the large number of farms and ranches, thankfully kept the development of residential housing to a minimum.

We passed over the bull killing sites. Each was a ranch, none so large or organized as Rufus Ford's, but each clearly was a cattle property.

As we passed over the fifth ranch, I hit the duplicator, and we began to retrace our route. I was tapping on the yoke to the beat of John Mellencamp's *Jack and Diane* in my head, when I realized something of a pattern. Earlier, when I'd made my map, I thought in terms of a circle. What I was seeing now was a bent teardrop shape, maybe like an enormous comma with the tail end pointing to a large swampy area covering the southern meeting point of Levy and Alachua Counties. It was called the Scrub.

Maybe the nucleus of the problem was somewhere deep in this swamp?

The Scrub is a swamp in the real sense of the word. It's populated with everything evolution has seen fit to leave behind. Many, multi-generational

93

locals believe the Scrub is haunted, spooky. I'd love to have a nickel for every time I heard some hunter tell the tale of a lost bloodhound in Cable's equivalent of the Bermuda Triangle. If I ever had to make an emergency landing, I sure didn't want to have to set down in the Scrub. Nevertheless, I swung the plane around and headed out over the swampy land.

When I was just thirty or so miles over the Scrub, I saw a series of long, rounded buildings. If my memory served me right, it was a former World War II supply depot. Maybe the perfect locale for a zombie gathering?

I needed my hands. I set the autopilot and asked Emma if she cared to watch the controls for a few minutes. We switched seats and I got a camera with a telephoto lens out of my bag. The autopilot took the plane in a long arc, hugging the edge of the buildings below. I shot nearly eighty frames. Not the expert in photography, I figured quantity was my best ally.

I finished with the pictures and took the controls back from Emma, I figured we would head home. I programmed in the numbers for the airstrip and let the plane do its thing. Many people don't realize flying isn't so complicated and I hope it stays that way. Who wants people who can't even drive a car whipping around in the air making the same mistakes they can't avoid on the ground?

Back at the house it was dinnertime. We always made a habit of grilling on our back porch on Sunday evenings. Instead of a hot tub, which I could never see why anyone in the South can stand with the heat and humidity, we have a large round cattle trough on the porch. We customarily fill it with water and lounge around while the food is cooking.

As I was sitting in the trough enjoying the cool water and a drink, Emma and Blue appeared in terrycloth white bathrobes. Emma carried a gallon jug of light blue liquid I soon realized was bubble bath and dumped the entire thing into the make-shift pool. Soon the tub was overflowing with dense fluffy bubbles. The bathrobes fell to the wooden deck in tandem and both ladies joined me. Blue looked at me with those butterfly eyelids and said, "How about a sandwich?"

I remember later having to feed Jake whatever it was we cooked on the grill. I didn't mind. Sometimes a sandwich can be very satisfying.

Chapter 26

The Prophet sat in a high-back wooden chair and looked out the window. The screw-up with the Hummers was a real problem. The events at the bridge had set things off. The men who failed him were worm food, but they were of little consequence, and his rage was still building. He needed to let some of the hot lava flow and felt the need for retribution more than ever.

He pressed an intercom. "Yes sir?"

The Prophet's voice was a low soothing hum, the kind which can garner attention even in its efficiency. "Send them in."

"Right away sir."

Two men entered the sparse room, their combat boots clicking on the stone floor, and stood at attention in front of the desk. It was Tito Salazar and Luis Alvarez—Daleen's replica. To everyone in the compound they were known as the Guardians.

Daleen kept looking out the window and said, "Please take a seat."

Alvarez said, "Sunshine State 666?" This was the code to initiate *Phase Two*.

The Prophet swirled the chair to face them. "Yes, gentlemen. The time is at hand. Our brothers who failed us have made it necessary to move our time line forward. Phase Two is to be carried out tonight. It must be swift and clean. It must deliver the message and still not lead any enemies to our gate. I trust you understand the gravity of the situation and will make any and all preparations to ensure the only possible outcome is in our favor. The Seekers have long been in remission, but our agenda will become clear with your success. There are to be no casualties on our part, there is to be no evidence left behind. Do you understand?"

Both men dropped to one knee and bowed their heads.

The Prophet uttered, "Good."

He turned the chair to stare out the window again.

Chapter 27

Monday

If the dark man was responsible for Jack, the game was now personal. I was a novice practitioner of Zen, and I knew it was wrong to take anything personally. But, I loved that little dog, damn the Zen.

Tom Goodrich was already into his breakfast when I arrived at the Lawless Diner. He hadn't seen fit to wait for me to eat. Whatever. Some people just don't listen when their mama is giving out etiquette advice for later in life. Tom looked up and grunted a hello. I nodded back.

I'd phoned ahead. As I was sitting down, Molly came out of the kitchen carrying my breakfast, putting it down on the table and giving me a knowing wink. Goodrich looked at me, then Molly, then back to me. "You must be one hell of a regular."

I passed over the comment and ate my breakfast like a prison camp refugee. When we'd both finished, I filled Goodrich in on what I had discovered so far—everything except the part about the suspect compound. When I told him about the Hummers, he tried to act less interested than he really was. I explained that even though I hadn't figured much out yet, I guessed that I must be onto something, because someone had tried to run me off the road.

He only snorted, "Well there's *that*."

I'm all too familiar with the frustrated and demanding client, especially in the early stages of an investigation. Goodrich wasn't a client, but he thought he was. He figured he was looking out for Ben. I didn't give a damn what he thought. I just wanted to keep him close. I wasn't sure he didn't know more than he was telling me.

I said, "Have you found your 'good man' to investigate the bull killings?"

Goodrich wiped his mouth with the napkin. "No. You probably already knew that though."

"I'll take the job."

Tom looked miffed. "I didn't offer."

"I'll solve this problem for you, and when I do, the Cattlemen's Association will pay me fifty thousand dollars. It's a small price to pay considering the millions in revenue already lost."

"You must be out of your mind."

"If for some reason I *don't* fix your problem, then you owe me nothing. I'll assume all risk and expenses."

Goodrich's face was strained and crimson tagged his cheeks. "I don't like you."

"I hear that sometimes."

"You are a cocky smartass, and I won't pay you one thin dime."

I wrote the name of a woman on a napkin, folded it, and pushed it over. Goodrich knew her well from The Construction Site. "You'll pay. If it makes you feel better, I'll be passing on the payment to Ben McCullers. Perhaps it'll offset some of his ranch expenses and ease his pain after losing Billy."

Goodrich smirked, picked up the napkin, read it, and crumpled it into a ball. Abruptly he seemed ready to burst with rage and humiliation. "You absolute asshole."

"I hear that sometimes. Best you stay away from The Construction Site for a while as well."

"I'll pay. But you still got to live here."

I flipped out a business card. "Now we both know where each other lives. I'll be coming 'round to collect."

The breakfast was satisfying. The conversation wasn't.

***

I headed over to the University. I figured it was better to see what my mushroom-picking friend could tell me before all of his brain turned into something resembling the underside of one of the fungi he loved.

I called Emma and asked her to find out from the registrar's office what classes the boy might be taking that afternoon. She told me he was in an art appreciation class over at the campus museum. Nothing like a little culture to make you feel better about yourself after a successful day of 'shroom picking.

I wandered around an exhibit titled the *Spiral of Extinction*. The underlying message was that we, the people of the planet, needed to consider our actions very carefully before building any more buildings or clearing any more land.

Brantley Snow came ambling from a classroom as I was pondering the similarity of this exhibit to a *Far Side* cartoon I'd read a few years earlier. The boy stopped for a drink at a water fountain. I walked up behind him and whispered, "Brant Snow?"

He turned around. It took a moment to recognize me. The fog from the day before lifted. He looked different, decked out in Ralph Lauren from head to toe. I guessed he was a prominent figure on the fraternity circuit. I immediately realized Brant Snow thought of me as low class, a country boy, who'd never reach the heights he believed inevitable for himself. There was also the hint of smugness that came from being in his own environment, not covered in cow shit from picking the mushrooms. He had an *air* about him.

He first tried the old standby. "What the hell do *you* want?"

"Brant, now that's not the kind of greeting I would expect after the hospitality I showed you yesterday when you were eating my mushrooms."

He looked around to see who might overhear. "I don't know who the hell you are or what you want, but you better leave me alone. Do you know who my father is?"

Father. I produced his driver's license and said, "I don't give a diddly fuck who your old man is. I told you I'd be coming by to ask some questions and here I am."

Fight or flight flashed across his face. He thought about making a scene. I could tell Brant was a lot more bark than bite. He shrugged his shoulders. "I don't know anything, and I'm not standing here having a silly-assed conversation with some farmer who thinks he's a cop."

"Ah, so you do remember me? Why don't we go over and have a little lunch, on me? I can ask a few questions, and your *father* never has to know you spend your Sunday afternoons picking mushrooms out of cow shit."

He wanted to come back with something smart, something threatening. But Brant Snow feared above all things the accusation I would make to his pops. I hated pulling the old "I'll tell your father" trump card, but I was kind of in a hurry and I couldn't keep verbally sparing. Besides, if this kept up, he probably *would* outsmart me and then I'd have to resort to a more primitive sort of motivation.

Brant Snow and I were enjoying Whoppers from the Burger King. He actually seemed like an all right kid once we got beyond the initial bravado. I finished my burger about the time Brant was putting the extra condiments on his. As a rule, I let people eat, but I could tell Brant would be a nibbler and I didn't have the patience.

"So Brant, what do you know about the Seekers?"

"Will this ever get back to me?"

"To be honest, it could. I'll try to keep you out of it, but some pretty hairy things are happening, and I might need you to tell someone else your story."

He toyed with a fry. I wanted to yell at him, *Eat the damn thing and stop playing with it.* It always bothers me when someone doesn't attack food. We are, after all, animals.

"They run the drugs in the county," he said. "Maybe more. I know the big cheese, some out of town big-shot—bought that old broken down whorehouse out on 245."

I was shocked, near speechless. Cannery Row had owned The Construction Site for as long as I could remember. "What makes you think he owns the whorehouse?"

"Hell, everybody knows that's where you go to get drugs. There wasn't a place anywhere you could score good shit until a couple of years ago when the Site became grand central good times."

"So, how do you know they had something to do with the bulls?"

"One of the local boys works for the Seekers dealing drugs; got all fucked up a few months back. He came with us to a fraternity party and started spouting off about this big secret organization he was a part of which was hell bent on cleaning out the farmers in the Cable area."

"What's his name?"

"Hell, I don't know his real name, but everybody called him Skeeter."

Great... *Skeeter.* That narrowed it down to just about a hundred good ole boys. "What else?"

"Sorry man, that's it. I don't run with those local cowboys. Hey, you aren't going to tell my dad about the mushrooms are you?"

"Not if the information holds out. And Brant, don't come picking on my property again ever, got it?"

Brant looked up, and I could see he hoped our paths would never cross again. I left him to finish his Whopper, which he still hadn't touched.

Chapter 28

I always enjoyed being on campus, even though the University of Florida wasn't my *alma mater*, and especially now that I didn't have to attend classes. College life was a time and place I always felt a tug to come back to. The library is my favorite part of the campus, where all manner of students were finding themselves in various and imaginative ways.

The green lawn called the Plaza surrounding the library is an open area with a few scattered oak trees providing shade. A small group of women were handing out flyers, mostly to other women. I tried to avoid an eager young female fixed on the sidewalk. A larger group of Hare Krishna followers were giving food to anyone brave enough to try it.

A crowd had gathered near the entrance to the main library and I wandered over to see what was so exciting. I wasn't disappointed. Two young men, in very different attire, were standing on old milk crates and were preaching to the crowd. It took a few minutes for me to get the gist of what was going on. The two were not working in concert but were eagerly presenting very different points of view.

On the milk crate to my left was Chuck, smartly dressed with a bow-tie, telling the crowd the evils the devil would surely bring upon them if they didn't mend their wicked ways. He would raise his voice and even rhyme to make his point. He read from the Bible, interpreting the scriptures to his own liking. On the other milk crate was Hate-Man. He was dressed in a long black gown and sported devil horns and a pitchfork. Each time Chuck read from the Bible, Hate-Man produced a tattered copy of Hustler magazine and try to drown out the scriptures with his own litany from the vivid, sexually explicit paragraphs of Hustler Forum. When Chuck mentioned God or Jesus, Hate-Man mirrored his comments, inserting instead the names of Big Bird and Mickey Mouse.

The crowd roared with laughter. I myself tried to be a little more enlightened, but actually it was funny as *hell*. Which is probably right where Hate-Man was headed with his "do not pass go, do not collect two hundred dollars" sign around his neck, and 666 tattooed to his forehead.

As I was leaning against a tree trying to conceal my laughter, Emma walked up from behind and looped her arm though mine. "Taking in the sights of our little corner of higher learning?"

Emma is the one I try to impress with my intellect. This little episode did nothing to further her view of me as enlightened. "Well they were just kinda there. I couldn't help noticing."

"They're out here every day. Most people think they're mortal enemies. But last year I saw them having a beer together at the Salty Dog Saloon. I think they've figured out salvation sells better when sin is threatening."

My image was shattered. I, like everyone else, wanted to believe these guys were out here unrehearsed, getting nasty with each other. More likely, they were practicing for what I was sure will be a very lucrative career on the evangelical circuit.

Emma still had a couple of classes to teach, but she walked me over to my truck. I felt like the big man on campus walking arm in arm with the sexy professor. I asked her, "You all right?" I meant Jack.

She forced a smile and gave me nod. It was as much as I could hope for.

Chapter 29

I was driving away from campus letting the facts I'd dug up congeal in my mind. I wasn't noticing my speed or my surroundings much, just driving by rote. In my rear view mirror the lights of a Cable Department of Law Enforcement car came to life. I know most of Blue's co-workers and most of them I think of as very good people doing a thankless and often dangerous job. Still, I always felt the dread everyone did when the lights come on behind you. I pulled into an empty parking lot of a long deserted Pic-And-Save and cut the engine. My eyes rolled when I saw Agent Jim Turner.

Turner doesn't much care for me and I feel pretty much the same about him. He's a short, stocky fellow with what we always referred to as "Small Man's Disease." In my opinion, he became a law officer so he could boost his ego and make up for his lack of stature. He also had the hots for Blue and was green with envy that I not only had her as a steady, but another very intelligent and easy on the eyes lady in Emma. Turner was *jonesing* for the opportunity to take me down a notch or two.

"You know the campus-wide speed limit is twenty-five miles per hour?" He asked with a smug grin under his aviator sunglasses.

"I did not know that," I said with my best Johnny Carson impersonation.

"How about stop signs? Did you know they're red, octagonal, and rather different from the yield signs, which are in an upside-down triangle?"

"You are quite the genius of geometry, Jimmy."

"Smartass, I was only going to deliver a message and give you a warning, but now I think I'll go ahead and give you a ticket for a moving violation. Two hundred bucks won't set you back much, but I'll feel better all the same."

"What's the message?"

"Knox wants to see you. You wait right there while I get my ticket book. Then you can be right on your way to see him."

"Tell you what Turner, I'll be on my way right now. If you feel the need to follow in hot pursuit in order to give me your little ticket, then you go right ahead. But instead, why don't you be a good fellow and walk your short ass back to the car, call your *boss* and tell him I'm on my way."

He was instantly smoldering, a stumpy fireplug, red in the face with rage and embarrassment. His tongue was tied in fury and instead of a snappy comeback, he snatched the aviators from his face and looked at me with genuine hate. I smiled a little "fuck you" smile and drove away. I would probably have to pay for that with Knox, and even Blue, but sometimes a little honesty is the best cure for Small Man's Disease.

Chapter 30

At the CDLE office I paced the floor, watched the clock. To pass the time, I made a mental list of the top ten geographical locations I wished to visit when time was available. I made it through the ruins of Machu Picchu, the Great Wall of China, the southern tip of the Aleutian Islands, and a beautiful valley in Madagascar I'd read about in National Geographic when Knox walked in. He didn't seem to be in a social mood.

"Cloud, what do you know about that mess out at the bridge the other day?"

"It was me they were after. I think it had something to do with the bull killings I've been looking into."

"No shit! I mean what do you *really* know?"

I measured the intensity in his eyes. I trusted Knox completely, but most often I kept a little of the story to myself. "I think there's more to this whole thing than some bulls getting killed. I think there might be a group, not local, behind it, but I haven't found any evidence yet."

"You make any connections between the bulls and women who've been killed?"

I shook my head

"No?"

"Was she…"

"Yeah. No ears, no teeth."

"How could it not be related?"

"We found weapons in the two Hummers. The dead guys were all wearing camouflage and seemed to be pretty well supplied. What do you make of that?"

"That fits the pattern of things I've uncovered."

"Not ready to tell me anything yet, huh?"

"Well Mac, there isn't really anything of value to tell just yet."

"When there is, can I expect you'll be, shall we say, forthcoming?"

"Tell me what *you* have found out?"

"You know that's information I can't divulge."

"I appreciate what you did with Emma and Blue out at the bridge the other day, but as it relates to this case, I'll show you mine when you show me yours."

"It truly is a pissing contest with you every single time. I could just lock you up until you tell me what I need to know."

"I suppose you could at that, but remember I know the Governor as well as you, hot shot. Besides, what the hell would that get you?"

"It damn sure would keep you from throwing gas on the fire which, I might add, you're very prone to do."

"Well, Boss man…"

"Stop fucking doing that Cloud. Why the hell do you have the need to agitate even the people on your side?"

"Sorry. You're right. But you know as well as I do that sometimes the only way to keep the forest safe is to do a little controlled burning from time to time."

"Don't wax Walden on me. You want to go out and stir things up, you make damn sure you do it on this side of the law."

I'd tired of our game of volley the bullshit. "Anything else?"

"You are one cocky bastard. I'll tell you one thing, if it weren't for Blue and me, most of the law around here would take every opportunity to stick your dick in the dirt. And you know what? I wouldn't stop them, not one little bit."

Sensing our meeting was over, at least the productive part, I got up to leave. He cleared his throat. "Is Emma all right?"

"I'm not sure. Why don't you give her a call, or better yet, go see her."

"You, my friend, are a dick head."

"Yeah. What about the survivor from the Old Oak Bridge?"

Knox got very serious. We were as tight as brothers, but like brothers, sometimes we didn't get along. "Don't. You hear what I'm saying? I've got two homicides to solve. The bulls are secondary. You leave that boy to me, got it?"

Knox watched me go to the door, then pretended there were more important things on his messy desk.

Chapter 31

UF Health Shands is the teaching hospital at the University. Blue had let slip the lone survivor of the Hummer incident was there and still in critical condition. Because he was the AIC of Cable, Knox was beholden to the law, and he'd have to wait until the boy was stable before he could legally talk to him. I didn't.

The emergency room entrance wasn't big, but it was chaotic. I waited until I saw several tearful parents and a pack of nurses walk through the door. I followed.

It took about twenty minutes of walking the halls of the hospital to find who I was looking for. He was big and slow and pushing a dingy mop around with very little purpose. I showed him the twenty in my hand. "I'm looking for a car wreck victim from Saturday."

He didn't look up, but reached out and took the twenty with a very quick hand. "They brought three in on Saturday."

"This one was early in the evening, not a student, might have been wearing camouflage fatigues."

He looked sideways at me, then down both sides of the hallway. "Yeah, I know the one." He continued mopping.

I pulled two ten-dollar bills from my pants pocket. I showed him both and handed him one. "What room?"

"212."

I gave him the other ten. "You didn't see me."

He moved the mop carelessly over my right boot. "Damn, I thought somebody was standing here talking to me. Reckon I was wrong. Janitors are often wrong."

***

I peeked in room 212 and saw a heavily bandaged young man in the bed. There was no one else in the room. I pushed the door open and locked it behind me. The man on the bed looked over with hazy, drugged eyes. I read his name off the chart hanging on the bed. Johnny Sanders, age twenty-six.

I took the emergency call device out of his hand and set it on the bedside table. His eyes strained to focus. I could see the pupils attempting to constrict. His right leg was in a cast with several metal objects protruding. It was elevated by a menagerie of cables and pulleys. He had a cast on one arm and a wrap of bandages covering most of his head. His nose had been broken and the black was seeping in around the fleshy tissue of his eyes. A wrap of bandage around his throat showed blood at the outer edges.

I leaned in close so he could see me. "Can you speak?"

He opened his mouth, but nothing came out. He shook his head. His eyes were wide now; the pupils were still out of whack.

"Do you work for a man who wears all black?"

No movement, except a tremble at the edge of his mouth. I pulled out my gun, the Python .357, and tossed it on his heaving chest.

"Do you?"

He nodded.

The monitors around him began to beep in rhythm. It would alert the nurses soon.

"Is he in the Cable Counties?"

I had his full attention now. I got another nod.

"Did he kill the bulls?"

Another nod.

"The women?"

He hesitated, true ugly fear in his loopy eyes. Then, another nod.

"Do you know why?"

110

He hesitated, then shook his head more vigorously than he'd nodded. So that was probably a lie.

The beeping of the monitors was nearly continuous. Something bumped up against the locked door.

"My name is Cloud. You remember it because your boss will want to know."

I took my pen from a breast pocket and yanked his casted arm close. I wrote, "Cloud Wuz Here!"

Chapter 32

Thirty Minutes Later

Bent Daleen entered the sliding doors of the hospital emergency room. He wore nondescript blue scrubs and a stethoscope around his neck. On the elevator he rode upward as canned crap Muzak rained down.

Room 212 was at the end of the long polished hallway. He moved with purpose but still managed to nod and smile at any passing nurses.

Four nurses and a doctor left the room as he was approaching. The doctor was spewing pontifications and the nurses were eagerly sopping it up. Daleen pushed through the door unnoticed.

He checked the chart. His information was correct. He made a mental note to eliminate the informant at the earliest possible opportunity. Loose ends and all.

Daleen removed a small glass jar from his pocket and looked at the serpent inside. Red rings married yellow rings, which in turn snuggled against black rings. He shook the jar agitating the snake, then grabbed the cast arm of the patient. Scribbled in black ink, the words 'Cloud Wuz Here!' stared back at him. A smile crept over his face.

He used a tongue depressor to make an opening between the cast and the patient's arm. He gave the jar another shake, opened the lid and let the snake sneak into the crevasse between cast and arm.

Before he could reach the door, a cacophony of beeps and whines erupted from the bank of monitors surrounding the bed.

Chapter 33

The Gallagher boys weren't telling all they knew. I'd known this for some time, probably since the first day, but now seemed a good time to follow up.

I stopped by Ballerini's store when I got to town and grabbed a can of pure cayenne pepper, two boxes of three-fifty-seven shells, a roll of duct tape, a squirt bottle, and a pack of water-proof matches. I placed the items in a bag, handed Mr. Ballerini a fifty-dollar bill, and walked left. No words were spoken and no receipt was written. In the reflection of the window as I left, I saw Ballerini put the fifty in his front jeans pocket. Mr. B was a Billy fan as well.

I headed to the Scrub. Seeing as how Knox and his agents had their hands full, I figured I might need a little help from other sources. *A man's got to know his limitations*, I thought, summoning the heralded words of Clint Eastwood. There are only a few men I trust. I called on Earl and Bean.

After about a dozen rings, which was typical, Earl picked up the phone, "Get-A-Head Taxidermy. 'You Snuff 'em, We Stuff 'em."

"I was looking for the president of the Britney Spears fan club," I said with a self-congratulatory smirk.

"Bean, it's for you," I heard Earl say, and could imagine the suppressed laughter.

"Who is it?" I heard Bean ask, bothered by the interruption.

"Hell I don't know. What do I look like, your secretary? It's some guy and he sounds pissed. I think it might be about money you owe that mail-out porno company."

I took the hint and tried to put on my best deep and serious collection company voice, just as I heard Bean say, "Aw shit."

Bean picked up the phone, "Hello?"

"Am I speaking to Mr. Israel Bean?"

"Yeah, this is Bean."

I knew I couldn't contain the laugh for long. "Mr. Bean, does your mother, a one Mary-Howard Bean, reside at this same number?"

"Yeah, what of it?"

"Well Mr. Bean, we've been trying to contact Mrs. Bean about a video tape she rented. It's a copy of *Farmer Fred Fondlesucks and the Sweet Ripe Tomatoes*. Do you know the tape I'm speaking of?"

"Screw you Cloud, and you too, Earl."

We both died with laughter.

"I'm gonna tell Mama you said she was a sweet ripe tomato."

"I said no such thing. What're you ladies up to?"

"I'm up to about six-six by two-sixty, and my little sister is an inch shorter and forty pounds fatter, what do you want?"

"I might need a little help. You two got some time?"

"Might. I'm working on a python some asshole from England sent us, and Earl's stuffing a wild boar's head for somebody in town. Is it something dangerous?"

"Could be. Might get bloody. There's a lot involved, and I need some backup in a quick, off-the-record kind of way."

"Anything. Whatcha want us to do?"

"Come and meet me at Mildred's. I'm gonna go check out a few things with the Gallagher boys, but if I need you, I want you close by." Mildred's was a grocery and dry goods store at the edge of the Scrub.

"We'll be there as soon as we can be. It'll take some time to finish up here, maybe an hour or two."

"No hurry. I just want you close, in case. Oh, and Bean, you fellas bring your huntin' tools."

"Never go anywhere without them, pardner."

***

I do my best thinking while driving. That's why I call the truck my office, also because I don't have an office of any other kind. Offices seem stagnant, they don't promote active thinking in my experience. You get all those pictures and knick-knacks on the walls and covering your desk, maybe a diploma, and you just get too comfortable.

I was out in the swamp. The road was old and cracked. Dead armadillos, raccoons, possums, and snakes littered the highway—road-kill leading me to some more wicked animals. A group of buzzards were feasting on something up ahead. I blew my horn. I'd once heard an old farmer tell Ben McCullers he'd surprised a flock of the winged scavengers on a back road. The birds didn't fly until he was too close and one went straight through his windshield. The dying buzzard flopped around the cab until the old man could pull over and jump out. He said he had to sell the truck 'cause he could never get the smell out.

The buzzards looked at me approaching and hopped to the side of the road. I guess they didn't want to lose their place in line. I pushed the diesel up to eighty and hurried on toward the Scrub.

***

The Scrub is about a hundred square miles of swamp. Palmetto bushes, cypress and cedar trees packed tight into any area not completely under water. Every once in a while I'd pass a large grove of pine trees. The lumber companies had dredged the land, clearing the old growth and setting up a canal system to control the water. The pines would grow for twenty years or so and then be harvested for pulpwood. It was big business in the Cable Counties. There probably wasn't one family who didn't have at least one soul doing the backbreaking work of logging pulpwood pines.

Spanish moss clung to the cypress and cedar trees lazily swaying to the occasional cough of wind. Alligators were at the top of the food chain within the Scrub. Nothing could challenge their dominance, save their one true natural predator: man.

I pulled into the old dry goods store, which must have been around since the turn of the previous century. Hand-painted signs on the road advertised ice, cold beer, and live bait. I parked at rhe diesel pump and began filling the twin tanks. An ancient woman, looking older than the store itself, stepped from the screen door and peered out at me. She didn't recognize the black truck and most likely wanted to make sure I looked to be a paying customer. She took a couple of hits from a corncob pipe as she watched. After a minute or so she nodded and I returned the greeting. She went back inside.

I finished filling the truck and went to the wooden porch surrounding the building. Four large open tanks hissed bubbles in brackish water. Hundreds of minnows scurried about below the surface. They were shiners, live bait used to attract largemouth bass or redfish. Most real fishermen didn't believe in using shiners, considered it cheating and the fishermen who used them to be lazy. I thought this was pretty accurate.

I dipped my hand into the water and opened my fingers wide. The shiners bumped and nibbled at my flesh.

In the store I gathered some food supplies I might need, if my stay in the Scrub turned out to be longer than expected. I put a block of cheddar cheese, some Saltine crackers, a dry paper bag of hot, spicy beef jerky and a twelve pack of Budweiser on the counter. The old woman sat in a rocking chair behind the counter and slowly got to her feet.

"How much diesel you pump?"

"One forty-two even," I replied.

She took another hit off the corncob pipe and the smoke seemed to disappear. She didn't exhale and even when she talked, the smoke never escaped. "Them saltine crackers is a little old, might be stale. You still want 'em?"

"I reckon I'll take 'em just the same. Feed 'em to the fish if I can't tolerate them."

"You must be headed to the Scrub, seeing as there ain't nothing else in the direction you're heading."

I considered the question. I didn't want to announce my presence to the Gallagher boys, and as far as I knew, this might be a long lost relative. But seeing she had figured out I really couldn't have any other destination, a lie would send more smoke signals than the truth. "Yeah, heading to the Scrub," I said.

"That's a mighty fancy truck you got there. Most people coming and going from the Scrub don't drive anything that new or nice. You visiting somebody?"

What the hell, I thought. When you're trying to find someone or something, most of the time you just have to put all your cards on the table and see how things turn out. Unlike their house trailer back near town, I didn't really know exactly where in the Scrub the Gallagher boys were, so I was eventually going to have to ask somebody. I might as well start with her. "Yeah, well, I'm looking for a couple of fella's might have come this way. Names are Amos and Gunnar Gallagher; you know them?"

"They friends of yours?"

"Friends, something like that. They have some information I need, and I thought I might ask them some questions. Have you seen them lately?"

"You're a big'un ain't you? Your name Cloud?"

I looked around to make sure the Gallaghers weren't slipping up on me from behind. "I'm Cloud. How might you have come by that information?"

"The Gallaghers. They was by here yesterday morning. Always stop on their way to the Scrub. They're a sorry couple of bastards. That's why I wanted to know if they're friends of yours. They always take whatever suits them and never pay a penny. This time they said some big ugly fella might come looking for them, name of Cloud, and if I was to see you to let 'em know."

Ugly? "You planning on letting them know?"

"Hell no, boy. Didn't you just hear me tell you they rob me every single time they come here? Fact is, I might want to hire you. I reckon they done something wrong to you or yours and you'd be going after them anyway. You look like you might just be able to smear their tired asses around one of those old palmetto bogs. All I want is what I got coming for all the gas, groceries, and beer they stole from me over the years. I've kept a tally and it's just about nine thousand dollars I figure they owe me, including the interest. I charged them forty percent seeing as they were loan sharking in reverse."

"Nine thousand dollars is a heap of money. This old store can't be taking in that much in a whole month, maybe two."

"You'd be surprised how much this old store takes in a month. It's the only one even close to the Scrub, and people who live there year round don't go to town much."

"Just the same, I don't know how comfortable I'd be taking your money."

"You look around and see a tired old lady with a broken down old store. That's what you see 'cause that's what I want people to see. I live a simple life, but I do just fine. My husband left me a thousand acres of timberland I lease out to the lumber companies, so don't you go worrying about me and my money. You want the job?"

"I'm not sure."

The old woman didn't bat an eye. "I'll give you ten percent of what you collect. That's nine hundred dollars. I don't care if it takes you ten minutes or ten months."

"I don't know whether the Gallaghers even *have* nine thousand dollars. Seeing their place back toward town, I can't imagine they have much of anything."

"You dim? Those boys been making moonshine and selling marijuana since they were kids. Their daddy was the same way. Besides, they got a truck, and I bet it's worth at least ten."

"You know where they are?"

"I know right where they are. Same old shack their daddy had down here for fifty years. So what, we got a deal?"

"What's your name?"

"Mildred Hayes. What do you say? Deal?"

"Well, I'll tell you what, Mildred. I'll pay my bill, and you throw in four or five flashlight batteries as a retainer and we'll have a deal."

"Done." Mildred stretched her hand across the counter and looked deep into my eyes to seal the deal. I shook a withered, calloused hand. She took the pipe from her teeth where it had been the whole time we'd been talking, and for the first time, she exhaled a long, dry puff of smoke.

Chapter 34

It's a good thing Mildred told me where to find the Gallagher boys' shack. If I hadn't run across her, I probably would've driven every back road and fence line in the Scrub to find it. As it is, I'm a lucky man. I hoped my luck would hold out.

I turned onto a narrow dirt road sheltered by a canopy of live oaks. Potholes filled with rainwater were more common than smooth ground. The branches slapped against the sides of the truck and mud splashed up onto the windshield. It was three o'clock in the afternoon and the sun had spent the whole day steaming up the swamp. A haze wafted through the splinters of light shining through the canopy. It was, as they say, a hundred and five in the shade.

I considered the possible ways of greeting the Gallaghers. I thought a silent guerilla move would probably be best—sneak up and surprise them with their pants down. What I really wanted to do was drive my truck right through their front door, grab the first one I saw, tie him to the truck bumper and drive through the swamp until he was ready to tell me what I wanted to know. Seeing as I didn't know the interior layout of their shack, I really couldn't risk blowing through the walls of the house and possibly killing both of them before I could ask my questions. No, better to walk softly and carry the big stick.

Mildred told me the shack was almost two miles off the black top down this dirt road. I pulled into a small stand of palm trees at about one and a half miles in. I got a small tactical backpack from my toolbox and assembled the few items I thought necessary to extract the information I would need. I packed the can of Cayenne pepper, a compact set of Steiner military binoculars, the rope, a Fenix Tactical flashlight, the role of duct tape, a squirt bottle of gasoline, the water proof matches, and a pair of pliers. I strapped on the shoulder holster with the Python .357 magnum and slid a Randall Fighting Knife onto my belt. Emptying a box of shells for the .357 into my hand, I pushed these into the pockets of my jeans. Two more boxes of shells went into the backpack. I strapped a Glock 26 to my ankle.

I grabbed the big hickory stick and headed down the dirt road, munching on a handful of beef jerky as I walked. Stopping after about a quarter mile, I found a tall live oak with limbs low and plentiful. I took out the binoculars and climbed into the branches.

The shack was barely a barn—old wooden boards nailed haphazardly in no particular order. The roof was tin, rusted and bent at the edges. Gunnar was in the yard, walking around eating something from a can. I could see the hunting dogs and the pit bull lazing under a tree with an ancient tire swing hanging from its branches. Amos must be in the shack, I thought.

I figured the dogs would notice me first, smell me, or hear some cracking branches. I left the tree and took the can of Cayenne pepper from the backpack, dumping the hot spice into my hands, first one then the other, the pepper starting to burn the skin of my palms.

Dogs don't get to choose their masters. If they could, they'd probably all live in Beverly Hills and get blueberry doggy massages every day at tea time. These poor bastards were getting the punishment for the sorry excuse for humans they belonged to. If there is a hell, I hoped these dogs would be one level up the food chain from their masters. I turned into the yard and the dogs leapt from their shady nap. All three barked and ran at me with frothing hate. Gunnar turned to see what the dogs were barking at. He wore overalls with no shirt and no shoes, one strap dangling at his side. He tossed the can of whatever he was eating on the ground. Something red painted the sides of his face. The dogs never broke stride.

I am a dog lover at heart, but I needed these particular dogs to be out of commission for a while, and I didn't want to hurt them permanently. Just as the pit bull, who reached me first, was in biting distance, I tossed the cayenne pepper into his face. He stopped as if he'd hit an anvil. The two hunting dogs followed and received the same. All three dogs were sneezing and yelping on the ground.

Gunnar was moving toward me, but stopped. "Hey, motherfucker, I've about had it with you picking on my dogs."

"Well, Moon Pie, why don't you come on over here and stick up for them?"

Gunnar took a step and threw a spoon at me, he missed by three feet. "Why don't you put the stick down and I'll do just that."

I dropped the stick and the pack to the ground and put an expression of *there, now what* on my face. He charged at me aiming for a belly-level tackle. He was slow. I stepped to the side and pushed him to the ground. He stood up with fury welling behind his eyes. "I'm gonna bend you up, Cloud." He took a looping roundhouse swing with his right hand. I ducked and shot a stiff right of my own, hitting him in the neck. He staggered back grabbing his throat with both hands. The dogs were still writhing around on the ground at his feet, the pit bull raking his face with his paws.

"Where's Amos?" I said.

Gunnar shook his head as he struggled to get the cramp from his windpipe. I stepped over to him and pushed his mushy, bearded face sending him backwards onto the ground. I pulled the Randall knife from my belt and cut the remaining strap of his overalls and the front bib fell, revealing his belly depository of Old Milwaukee.

Amos rounded the side of the shack. He held a coiled bullwhip which he unwound and snapped with some expertise. "Cloud, you had this coming for a long time. I'm gonna take a pound of hide off your ass with this here whip."

I grabbed Gunnar by his greasy hair and pulled him to a standing position. His overalls fell to his ankles. I muscled a hard right into his kidney and he fell face first. I looked back towards Amos and gave him my satisfied smile, then took a couple of steps towards him. He cracked the whip as if in warning, maybe a practice shot.

"I heard you boys got religion—a bunch of bull killers and goat fuckers or something."

Amos sneered, but I'd hit a nerve. He popped the whip just to my right, measuring my reaction.

He said, "That's the problem with you, asshole. You got no religion. You don't *believe* in anything."

"Why that's just not true. What an ugly thing to say. I believe in equal opportunity ass whippings for all sorry ass scum of the earth. What do you know about some wild band of hippie-freak bull killers?"

Familiarity showed on his face and he tried to disguise it with another sneer. "I don't know anything about no Seekers and such."

"Well, we'll just have to see about that the hard way, I reckon."

Amos cracked the whip, and I felt it sting my right hip. He already had the whip swirling above his head like a lasso ready for the throw. "How does that grab you, sissy boy?"

Acid built in my throat with a twang of adrenaline and I tasted rage at the back of my tongue and through my nostrils. I wanted to pull the .357, but I needed information. These boys were just the means to an end. I circled behind Gunnar, putting him between his brother and me. Sweat was running down my arms and the knife handle felt slick in my hand.

Amos was wearing a filthy, nondescript cap, which he reached up and turned around backwards. Now he was getting down to business. He popped the whip, and I felt my cheek open. I touched it and looked at the blood on my fingers. If it hadn't been for the information I needed, I would have shot him dead right there.

"Looks like you cut yourself shaving there, pussy boy."

I took several quick steps towards him, and this time when the whip came, it wrapped around my waist. I wound the whip around my hand and yanked Amos toward me. The whip was tethered to his wrist with a loop of cowhide, and he stumbled forward. My training taught me to save my hands. I elbowed him in the nose and could feel the bone and cartilage smash behind the impact. He floundered, trying to throw the loop off his hand, while at the same time trying to inspect the damage to his nose with his other hand. I cracked the top of his head with the knife butt, and he sunk to his knees. I shoved him on his belly and used the small end of the whip to tie his hands behind his back. He lay on the ground, blood gushing from his broken nose.

Gunnar was just getting to his feet. I hit him a one, two combination to the gut and head-butted him in the face. His nose exploded too, soaking both of us in his blood. I took the rope from the pack and tied his hands behind his back. The dogs were still in a bad way. I grabbed them one at a time and threw them into a water trough. It was only a foot and half deep so the dogs could relieve the pain and still get out on their own.

They each jumped from the trough and shook vigorously, seemingly baptized in good common sense. They looked up at me as if to ask, "what now?" I dumped the sack of beef jerky on the ground. The dogs looked quizzically for a moment, gulped a mouthful of jerky, and headed back to the napping tree.

Chapter 35

Both the boys were out cold. Both were breathing—that was good.

I kicked in the door of the shack. The inside was sparse in furnishings, but rich with smell. There was an old couch piled with foul blankets and dingy soiled pillows. In the kitchen the counters were covered with unwashed pans reeking of dried, molding food. Several opened, half-eaten cans of chili sat on the edge of the table near a trashcan that had spilled over and coughed up the remains of many dinners past. I pushed into the one bedroom and gagged at the stench. These boys definitely needed to work on their hygiene. I didn't want to have to touch anything and was relieved to see two olive-drab camo fatigue tops with the moon insignia Tree Raulerson described. Well, at least I knew the boys were converts to the new religion, the so-called Seekers.

There didn't seem to be a bathroom. Just as well. I might have contracted something deadly from the faucet handles. I went back outside, found a garden hose and washed the blood from my face and hands.

The dogs waddled over to where I was taking my whore bath and lapped at the water. I believe they'd seen the light. I might just have made a few new friends.

I hauled the Gallagher boys over to the cow trough and propped them against it and each other. They still had their hands tied behind their backs. I cut a piece of rope and bound their feet as well. The possibilities for extracting the information danced in my head. I was fairly giddy at the thought of them resisting my inquiries. Time was a factor. I needed to get back to Knox with something to keep him at bay, so I decided the long version of information retrieval was out. Best to get right to it.

***

I admit now, I may have gone a little overboard. I still had an unpatched hole in the center of my heart where Jack used to be, and I didn't take too kindly to being run off the road with my women in tow.

"Ladies," I said, spraying their faces with the garden hose. They mumbled and opened their eyes. Groggy and full of pain, recognition of their predicament slid across their faces. I continued to spray them with the hose until they were gagging and spitting the water back. I felt I had their full attention.

"What I want is information. After I've gotten what I want, I'll take you to the sheriff. I assume he'll flush your sorry asses into one or the other of our fine state prisons. That's if the FBI doesn't take you from him and send you to be the sponge bath maids to some big, hairy-assed murderer.

"You may wonder what your incentive is to give me information, when you can only expect to be wards of the prison system in either case. I will tell you. If you don't tell me what I want to know, rest assured you will not leave the Scrub alive. If it takes *longer* than I want, you'll be missing body parts when you see civilization again. Capeesh?"

They just looked at each other with bug eyes.

"Do you understand?" I said.

Amos opened his mouth to give what I guessed might be a derogatory remark, and I kicked him in the forehead, snapping his head back into the galvanized steel trough.

Gunnar said, "Listen motherfucker, we now serve a higher power. If you think you gonna get anything out of us, you're crazy as a sprayed roach."

Sprayed roach? "Good, very good. I was hoping you would choose to do this the hard way. Unfortunately, I'm in a big hurry, so I can't toy with you and your higher power."

I produced a gallon-size glass jar I'd found among the clutter of the nasty kitchen and stuck a large funnel which had been wedged into the gas tank of a broken down lawn mower into the top. I then showed them a bucket full of sand I'd scraped up. "I'm going to pour this sand into this funnel. When the sand is gone I will kill one of you. Then I will repeat the process. I figure you have five, maybe six minutes, tops. While the sand is doing its work, I'll try and help your memory as best I can. Okeydokey? Good, I'm glad we understand each other."

"Many people of faith were persecuted for their beliefs," Amos croaked. "We're believers. The Seekers are a righteous group who know what God has commanded. We won't tell you anything that'll hurt our cause."

These boys were almost too dumb. I reached forward and snipped Amos's right earlobe with the knife. He wailed in pain and disbelief. I poured the funnel full of sand. The grains began to drop into the glass. "Are the Seekers responsible for killing the bulls?"

Gunnar's lower lip trembled, and I thought he might end our game right here and now. But Amos shrieked at him, "Don't tell this sorry cocksucker nothing, brother."

I sensed Gunnar was the weaker of the two. I pulled the .357 and shot two holes into the cow trough, one on either side of his head. The moldy water poured from the trough, and Gunnar began to cry.

By the time the sand ran out, each man was missing a toenail and both had pissed their pants. But I had the information I needed.

***

The Gallaghers had gotten wrapped up in the Seekers for the same reason they had gotten involved with the Klan a decade back. Same reason they hung out with the trouble-makers in school—they just couldn't help it. For poor, white wannabees in a small country town, everything wicked this way comes. If the initiation to the Seekers had been to run through town naked with devil's masks and pitchforks, I believe they would have done just that. These boys just wanted to be part of something—anything.

Now they could be part of the "missing toenail" or the "I hate Cloud" fan club.

I pulled my truck up next to the trough and looked almost sympathetically at the boys. They were trash, and now they were going to prison. They probably had known it would turn out like this one day. I hear there are all kinds of clubs to join in prison, too.

I made sure the boys' hands and feet were tied real tight and wound a couple turns of duct tape around the missing toenails. Then I heaved them over into the back of the truck one at a time. I told them to lay low and keep quiet, then showed them the roll of duct tape. I think they got the message.

I had one final question for the boys, and even though I didn't think they had the loot, I felt I should ask. "Boys, y'all owe Mildred down at the store some money. Do you have any cash?" The boys shook their head in unison. Well, I wasn't going to go through the nasty crap in that house looking for it, not even for nine hundred dollars. Country boys love their trucks and usually keep what's important to them somewhere close. I decided to do a quick check of the truck, and if the money wasn't there I'd take the keys to Mildred and she could sell it.

But low and behold, when I pulled the driver's seat forward there was an old cigar box full of cash. I grabbed the box and climbed into the cab of my truck. The Gallagher's seemed defeated and didn't say a thing.

Back on the road I left a message for Knox. I relayed some of what I found out from the Gallaghers. Just after Amos was separated from his toenail, he confessed the Seekers had a compound down here in the Scrub. He said there were about a hundred members in this chapter of the Seekers, but millions worldwide. *Yeah right.* He said they didn't know the whole plan, which I believed, but they were supposed to feed some sugar cubes to Mr. McCullers' cows and to kill Billy as their initiation into the Seekers. They said the sugar cubes had something in them which would make the cows sick, but they didn't know what it was.

I asked if it was some kind of disease, and Gunnar popped his tongue as the light bulb went on. "That's it," he said, but he had no idea what it was. He said this chapter covered the Cable Counties and the faithful were going to be giving cows in all of them the tainted sugar cubes. The Seekers held a vigil once per month, on the full moon, at the compound. Amos said about thirty of them lived there full time. I mentally doubled his estimate.

I asked about weapons. He said they were more of a peaceful group. I didn't believe this and summoned visions of Waco and Ruby Ridge. They said the main event, the multi-county sugar-cube orgy, was to happen in three days. I cut this time in half to make it more believable too.

Chapter 36

I parked the truck at the diesel pump in front of Mildred's. The store seemed empty, but it was like that when I was there before. I slopped some dingy water from a bucket on my windshield and walked towards the store. One of the Gallaghers yelled from the back of the pickup, "Hey Cloud, bring us something to drink, why doncha."

I looked back over my shoulder with the answer in my eyes. They both slouched back into the bed of the truck. I got the feeling something was wrong as I went up the steps, but I ignored it. Bad move on my part.

The cowbell above the door clanged, the screen door slammed behind me. I could hear a television in the background, some midday talk show with guests yelling at each other and throwing chairs. I called out to Mildred. She didn't answer. I began to search the store, looking around every isle and counter, *nothing*. I moved toward the sound of the television and looked into an office behind the counter.

There was Mildred, bound and gagged, her hands behind her and a thick swatch of tape across her mouth. Her eyes were wide with fear. No, it was a *warning*.

Then someone hit me in the back of the head and Fourth of July fireworks exploded in front of my eyes.

***

I woke up to *Korn* blaring from the radio on the counter. I was tied to a chair and the Gallagher brothers were standing in front pissing on me, trying to arch the stream up to my face. Four guys with camo masks and a half moon stitched on the front of their shirts stood behind them. Mildred was in the corner, still in *her* chair, still bound and gagged, her eyes burning with hate. They'd tipped her back so her feet couldn't touch the ground. If she squirmed, she'd fall.

Gunnar Gallagher was fairly light with glee. "Bet you can't piss in his eye, brother."

Amos responded, "Bet you a case of Old Milwaukee I can, brother."

Both men strained their hips forward and I was drenched in urine. One of the masked men moved forward and shoved the brothers aside. They were really through at that point anyway.

"The Prophet says you need to desist. We have holy business to do and you are discouraging it." The language and tone weren't local. I couldn't place it.

I strained at the bindings behind my back. "Did the Phallic tell you fellas to let the Gallaghers baptize me like this?"

Gunnar struck forward and hit me across the chin with his elbow. I saw stars. The masked man shoved him aside and looked at him with dire consequences. Gunnar dipped his head.

"People say you are a philosopher, an amateur humorist, always poking your nose where it doesn't belong."

"It's a nice nose, only broken three times, twice while head butting a coward like you."

The mask smiled, revealing green teeth—not really green, but it seemed that way. "I thought you wouldn't be persuaded by a rational argument, so we're taking the old woman with us, and the same thing is gonna happen to her as all those bulls. As for *you*," his tone changed to mimic my country dialect, "we're just going to have ourselves a good old fashioned barbecue."

He turned to the other masked men and nodded. They started soaking everything in the store with cans of gasoline.

"Man is evil and has no chance for salvation save his own initiative," he said.

"Nice quote there, wizard," I said.

130

"You just don't know when to shut up, do you there, boy?"

"I was blessed with the forked tongue."

"Well, you and your forked tongue can roast in hell in about five minutes. Enjoy the after-life, tough guy."

The others left the building and the one who'd spoken looked at the Gallagher boys and nodded toward the door. The Gallaghers stood still and looked at the mask with pleading eyes.

"C'mon brother, let us mess this sissy fucker up just a little, to make up for what he done to us."

The mask stepped forward and slapped them both, sending them stumbling toward the door. Then he leaned in close to my face and said, "I really don't even believe in all this cow killing and freak-show mumbo jumbo. I just like the part where I get to kill people like you."

"A man should enjoy his work," I said with a smirk.

"Smartass to the end. No problem, I'm going to visit your professor lady later tonight. How does that grab you?"

I looked at him with laser hate. I couldn't do anything, and nothing came to mind to say, so I just smiled as if I didn't care. He took a Zippo lighter from his pocket and scratched it lit. He slapped my cheek playfully and threw the lighter toward the back of the store.

The whole world caught fire.

Chapter 37

When a crisis emerges I've always had an innate ability to find the calm. It's not something I consciously seek; it just naturally happens. I get mad just like everyone else, maybe even with a little more intensity, but somewhere sometime after the storm has passed in front of my eyes a tranquil peace takes over. I now found myself in that position. I'll find another plane to set my mind on and the subconscious part of my brain usually knows what to do.

I focused on the concept of cowardice, even as my hands were guided by some unconscious effort to free themselves. In my experience, cowardice does not always manifest itself in the traditional running away format, but often in a bullying effort. The Gallagher boys and the masked men probably knew I was on a righteous path, so they came in force to bully and subdue what they felt as a threat. It's like when you're speaking to someone on the phone and you have a disagreement. I find most people try to be ten feet tall over the phone, but in person they handle matters no better than a child.

The store was burning quickly. I wasn't sure even if I could get my hands free, that I could get out of the building before it was completely consumed. As my hands worked with a mind of their own and my brain debated the concepts of boldness and cowardice, I saw cans of motor oil pop from the shelves, paint boiling on the outside ready to turn into miniature missiles, if they came apart. Shelves of food and dry goods turned brown and the acrid smoke engulfed my face.

To my right, a four-drawer filing cabinet sat undisturbed so far. Taped to

the side was a cartoon-drawing of a large pond bird trying to eat a huge
bullfrog. The frog had reached out with his front hands and was throttling
the bird even as the bird was swallowing his head. The caption at the bottom
of the cartoon read, "Never, ever give up!" Good advice at a time like this.
I'm sure Mildred didn't have quite this scenario in mind when she taped that
cartoon in place. Or maybe she did—she seemed like a tough gal.

I decided to get a little lower. Maybe the smoke wouldn't be so bad close
to the floor. I threw all my weight backwards and the chair teetered and fell
sideways towards the filing cabinet, slamming my face into the dusty floor. I
licked a trickle of blood at the side of my mouth and started losing
consciousness. In a few moments it wouldn't matter how much I struggled.
My eyelids were heavy, and as they narrowed to slits, the door exploded
inward.

It wasn't the fire. It was Earl and Bean.

Both men were carrying five gallon buckets and looking frantically
around. I yelled, but it came out muffled and weak. It was enough. They
turned and saw me lying on the floor. The last thing I saw was Earl heaving
the bucket of water in my direction. It was full of little fish—they'd gotten
the water from the tanks on the porch. Ten gallons of briny water, full of live
bait fish, splashed all over my body.

***

I woke up coughing and hacking, lying in the dirt outside the store. A column
of smoke billowed up a hundred yards high. The store was burning intensely
and would be ash and earth in a matter of minutes. Earl leaned over me and
yelled to Bean, "Told you he wasn't dead. Can't kill a pig-headed bastard like
him with a little fire."

Bean dropped an old army blanket over me and grinned as wide as a
sunrise. "Ya had us worried there for a minute, you sorry injun bastard."

I coughed more, and a thick string of mostly spit dribbled from my chin
to the ground. "I been telling you our whole lives that *injun* is a gross
insensitive term." With that I just smiled up at the two huge faces bending
over me.

Darkness gathered around us and the mosquitoes were out in force. The boys erected a cot they obviously had purchased at a surplus Army/Navy store. When I attempted to get up and walk, Bean pushed me back down before cradling me in his huge arms and lifting me off the ground. I fluttered my eyelids. "Bean, I didn't know you cared."

"Shut up little man, you ain't heavy, and I only care a tiny bit."

He laid me on the cot. "Volunteer fire department don't come out this far. They asked if there was any chance the fire would reach the timber stands. When I told them no, well, they just kinda laughed and said they'd send someone in the morning."

Earl had a six-pack of Old Milwaukee and a bottle of Jim Beam. He tossed the six-pack to Bean and opened the bottle. He raised the bottle and saluted, "Here's to backyard Bar-B-Qs, food worth eating, and Emma and Blue." He put the bottle to his lips and I saw several bubbles slink along the neck before he took it down. He passed the bottle to Bean who did the same, then wiped his mouth on his shirtsleeve.

Bean came over to me with the bottle asking, "You want I should hold your head?"

"Only if you're talking about the little one."

He rolled his eyes. "I guess he's feeling better." He passed me the bottle and I took a long slow pull, propping myself up on an elbow.

I needed to lighten the moment. "Two country boys, I think their names were Earl and Bean..." I started.

Earl cut in, "Aw shit, here he goes."

I looked insulted. "Anyway, two country boys, Earl and Bean were walking down a back road." Both of the men leaned in, hungry for the funny part. "They saw an old cur dog sitting by the fence licking himself. Just bathing his ass and balls. Earl said, 'I wish I could do that.' To which Bean replied, 'Unh huh, that dog would biiiiite you."

Both men rolled with laughter, which made my heart lift just a little. Earl looked at Bean. "I guess you were right. I think he's coming around."

***

134

When I went off to the Military Academy, both Earl and Bean enlisted in the Army. They'd been raised by Mama Bean to believe every man owed something to his country. Model soldiers, both rose up the ranks to Sergeant. They fought in the Desert Wars and distinguished themselves in different ways. Funny as it may seem, the war was what made them get out. I heard Earl tell his Mama one day, "The fighting was all right, but there were just too many damn rules and the money was no good."

My encounter with the masked men from the Seekers left me a little humbled. I knew I was no superhero, but I really didn't anticipate the ordeal I'd just been through. I was going to have to sharpen up and depend a little less on just whipping everyone's ass.

I asked Earl to bring my phone and note pad from the truck. Shifting an old bucket around to the side of the cot, I made a make-shift desk. When Earl returned, I saw I had two messages, one from Emma and one from Knox. I called Blue and got no answer. I tried Emma and she picked up on the third ring. "Hey babe, everything all right?" I held my breath.

"Everything's fine, where are you?"

"Down in the Scrub. Is Blue home?"

"Yeah, she's right here."

"Let me talk to her please."

Blue came on. "Cloud, where are you?"

"I'm in the Scrub. Earl and Bean are with me and everything is all right. I want for you to be mighty careful tonight 'cause one of these bull killers made a threat."

"Do you think it's serious?"

"Serious enough for you to call Mac and tell him what I've told you."

"Cloud, what's happening?"

"I don't know exactly, but make sure you and Emma stay close to the house and call Mac, okay? I'll be there as soon as I can."

Chapter 38

On a woven rug inside his quarters Daleen finished his daily yoga regime. Some he'd learned from the Institute, some he'd fashioned from his own research and practice.

A knock at the door interrupted his final breathing exercise. He said, "Enter."

A lone Seeker warrior, the leader of the group who incinerated the old woman's store, entered and held steady and silent.

Daleen didn't move, his back facing the new arrival. "Speak."

"My prophet, the interloper has been neutralized."

"How?"

"Beaten, bound, and burned."

"You saw this happen?"

"I lit the fire myself."

Daleen rolled his neck. "You may leave."

The Seeker loyalist backed through the door, closing it.

Daleen raised his head and smiled.

Chapter 39

I finished a fit of more jagged coughing and spit a dark glob of phlegm on an ant bed. The phone was ringing on the other end.

"Mac Knox."

"It's Cloud."

"'Bout time, you ass. I just got off the phone with Blue."

"You making any headway on the *people* killer end?"

"I can tell you one thing, somebody shoved a coral snake in the cast of our surviving Hummer runner. He's dead. What do you know about that?"

"Red and yella' kill a fella'."

"Asshole. Did you do this?"

"No."

"No? The timing is highly coincidental."

"No, I wouldn't use a snake. Bad for the snake."

"Huh, maybe true, but you'd damn sure know how."

"You got a leak."

"Bullshit."

"You been away, suspended. I'm just telling you that you got a leak in your department."

Knox heaved a long impatient sigh. "What in the hell makes—"

"Find the leak and tie if off."

"Who the hell are you to tell me what to do?"

I clicked the phone dead.

Chapter 40

Earl, Bean and I were riding toward The Construction Site in my truck and listening to the macho rock of Chris Rea. Rea's voice was sticky and seductive, at the same time fulfilling with ten-foot tall maleness.

I'd used the water hose out back and a bar of Ivory soap to cleanse myself of the Gallagher baptism. A spare set of jeans and a Parrot Head t-shirt were in the toolbox. I made do.

The boys had been riding in silence enjoying the music, when Bean finally said, "What're we looking for at the Site?"

"I really don't know. I was over there the other night and things were different. Cannery was actually acting as if she was afraid of something. Then this dark man showed up and the whole place seemed to tremble. I was supposed to talk the next day with one of Cannery's girls but… well things happened. Maybe I can follow up tonight."

"This have something to do with the bulls?" Earl asked.

"It might. I also had a little run-in with some boys down at the Old Oak Bridge. I think these things might be connected."

"Whatcha want us to do?"

"Just stand around being big, mean, and ugly. That should be pretty easy for you two."

Earl looked over at Bean and spoke as if I weren't there. "I tell you what, Bean. You be the big one, I'll take care of mean, and we'll leave *ugly* to our old buddy Cloud, whatcha think?"

Bean, always a step behind when the conversation turned to hell giving, wrinkled his forehead and could only muster, "Yeah Cloud, you're ugly."

I smiled and we pulled into the parking lot. It was a tinge early for things to get going at The Construction Site. Most people were just arriving. Still, my truck was anonymous among the other pickups.

We went through the same entry routine I had a few nights before. When we reached the bar room I looked over at Bean and saw a familiar kid-in-a-candy store grin on his face. No matter how many times Bean sees scantily-clad woman, he always has the same poor dumb country boy stance, his hands buried deep in his pockets and ready to spew forth an "Aw shucks" the moment one of the women shows him some attention.

We sat there a few minutes before the twin waitresses came to our table. One of them seemed to have a little more makeup around the eyes and the other was wearing shades. That little warning light went off in my head and I almost asked who'd hit them, before they even took our drink order. I'm sure the boys didn't notice anything or they would have started conducting a body cavity search of everyone in the room for evidence of who might have laid a hand on such lovely women. Hitting women is the work of the most cowardly lumps of shit on the planet, as I'm sure my friends would have pointed out to the person responsible for the ladies' injuries.

As the twins were leaving, Cannery Row appeared at our table. Before I could greet her with my customary pulling out of the chair, she leaned down and said quietly, "You should just get up and leave as fast as possible."

The smile faded and I got my back up. "What the hell is going on 'round here, Cannery? First, you almost surely lied to me the other night, then shooed me out the door. Then, tonight we don't even have one drink and you're trying to get rid of me again. I might get the feeling you aren't quite as sweet on me as you've professed these many years."

"This isn't a game. There are things going on around here you'd justa soon be steering clear of."

"Well I'm not steering clear of anything. In fact, I'm just about to drive head-first into them at light speed. If you're in trouble, I can help."

"Cloud, your heart has always been ten sizes bigger than your head. This thing is way bigger than you. And no matter how tough you feel with Earl and Bean riding shotgun, it won't be enough."

"What's going on behind that green door?"

All the blood left her face. "I want for you boys to leave right now."

"Well we aren't leaving and if you don't start coming across with some answers which make me feel better about your safety and that no really bad shit is going on here, I'm going to walk straight through that green door."

Her eyes were wet, pleading and scared. "Please don't. It won't be good for you, and it could mean the end for me."

The twin waitresses returned with the drinks and Cannery shot them a look that meant get the hell out of here. I was between the proverbial rock and a mud hole. I needed to get more out of this visit, but I didn't want to put Cannery or her girls in any danger. But I say, *when in doubt, stir things up*.

"Cannery, tell me right now what the trouble is or I'm going to put my size twelve through that door and up somebody's ass on the other side."

"Just give me another day. Come by tomorrow and I'll tell you anything you need to know. Do it for me, Cloud."

I know now I should have trusted my gut. I should have kicked that door in and dragged the bastards behind it out into the street and made them tell me what was what. But I didn't. I succumbed to the pleading eyes of my old friend, Cannery Row.

It was the last time I saw her alive.

Chapter 41

The next morning I woke up to Emma's face leaning over me in bed. She looked worried and anxious. "What's up?" I asked.

"It's Blue. She's on the phone and it's bad."

Cold gut nausea started in my stomach and worked up through my face, burning my sinuses like I had been punched a good one in the nose. "Is she all right? Is she hurt?"

Emma's eyes moistened and her body language almost made me grab her by the shoulders. "Blue's okay, but it's bad. Here, take the phone."

I snatched the phone. "Blue, you okay?"

The normal hard-charging cockiness was gone from her voice. "I'm fine. I'm out at The Construction Site Bar and Grill. Cannery Row and a few others are dead. The place has been burned to the ground."

Black rage leapt behind my eyes. I felt a spike divide the parts of my brain between emotions and reason. "I was just there last night..."

"I know. I'm sorry. I know she was your friend. Don't fly off the handle and go doing anything you'll regret. Just let me see what I can find out and I'll call you."

***

I was in the truck ten minutes later trying to get a handle on my anger and guilt. I knew what I should have done the night before. The thought kept running through my brain, *She's dead because of you. She paid the price for your hesitancy. You blinked and someone swatted her like a fly. Live with it tough guy, live with it today and every goddamn day for the rest of your life. If you come to the line meaning to do business, then by God, business better get done.*

I remembered a lesson my dad tried to teach me. It was one of the only things I remembered about him before he left. We were sitting in the living room of our old trailer and he was leaning across with a greasy smile and bourbon breath. He grabbed a pencil and interlaced it through his thick fingers, raised his hand and brought it down on his knee with a loud pop. The pencil shattered, and it looked as if he had broken a fence post instead of a pencil. "Now you try it."

He handed me another pencil and shakily I put it between my five-year-old bird-feather fingers. I looked at him for support. He only looked back with anticipation and a taunting air. "Do it!"

I didn't want to do it and I was pretty sure I *couldn't* do it. I raised my hand intending to bring it down hard, but I hesitated. I brought my hand down weakly and barely popped my knee. The ensuing crack was not from the pencil, but from my finger. The greasy smile reappeared on my dad's face and a satisfied look. He said, "Look how much bigger, stronger, and smarter I am. You're a sissy, Cloud. A pussy. You don't have the guts to break a goddamn pencil. I'll tell your mother to buy you a dress today, and tomorrow you'll wear it, ya little fruit."

I didn't end up having to wear a dress, but I did wear the shame of a broken finger for six weeks or so. Now I would be wearing that same dress of guilt and shame for my friend, Cannery Row.

I wheeled into the gravel drive in front of Earl and Bean's taxidermy shop. I jumped from the truck, my mind thick with self-hatred and some left over for whoever did this. I banged through the door and both of the boys looked up. "I need to see both of you out back," I said, locking the front door and turning the sign in the window to "Closed."

This had happened a time or two before, when one of us had some tragedy or was boiling over with fury. They knew what I'd meant and followed me out the back door to the dirt lot behind the shop. I started lacing on sixteen-ounce boxing gloves. Earl wanted to put his big arm around my shoulder and ask what was wrong, but he knew that would come later. Right now I needed *this*.

Bean was putting on the other set of gloves, but Earl took them from him, a silent message passing between them. Nobody had ever beaten Bean in a fight of any kind, with gloves, bare knuckles, or even knives. Earl would take the lumps, because he knew Bean would half kill me in my present state of mind.

Still, Earl first wanted to try and comfort his friend. I popped him in the face with a quick right jab. His eyes changed and the mood was set. "If that's what you need, then that's *just* what I'll give you."

It wasn't the *me* I could ever be proud of. I fought my friend with an intent just this side of trying to cause permanent damage. I hit him hard, fast and continuously. When I saw I'd hurt him, I dug deeper and pushed the feelings of pity to that place of greasy smiles and threatened dresses. When he fell, I punched him in the back of the head. I was in the process of trying to kick him, when a huge hand slammed into my chest. It was Bean.

"That's enough, Cloud. You don't mean it. You're hurting him."

Quick as a snake, I slammed an overhand right into Bean's face. My hand met stone through the glove, and the big man just stood there. I reared back to bury my fist into his big dumb-looking face again, but I didn't have a chance. Bean hit me one time and the lights went out in Cable County.

I woke up twenty minutes later lying on the floor of the kitchen. There was a wet rag on my head, and Earl and Bean's mom was tending to Earl's face while she hummed a soothing tune.

Mama Bean finished patching up Earl's face and then told the boys to go on back to the shop. She needed to talk to me. A combined five hundred and seventy pounds of mean-ass country boy did just what their mama said, leaving the two of us alone in the room.

Mama Bean came over and turned the rag on my forehead letting the cool side rest deliciously over my troubled brain. She wasn't mad, even though I can't imagine why. I just tried to really hurt her natural born son. I believe it could have been she saw me in the same light as her boys and with the same affection. She'd bandaged and kissed our hurts away our whole lives. What should change now that we were men?

"What's wrong, Baby Child?"

I was still shell-shocked from Bean's sledgehammer fist. I was also hurting inside with an intensity ten sledgehammers couldn't have inflicted on my heart. Despite all of that, I didn't want to tell her. I didn't want to need someone to be there for me. Even more, I wanted no pity. But, I guess no matter what I wanted, I needed the understanding and the unconditional love of this old woman. I told her about Cannery Row and my role in her death.

"You always been the responsible one, Cloud. The one who thought he could control everything. You're always thinking everything what went wrong was *your* fault. I remember when you boys were in grade school and Bean earned a poor report card. *You* actually brought the card to me as if it was in some way your responsibility to make sure his grades were up to snuff. You got to get this torture outta your soul. You got to start realizing *life* has its own agenda. You can change most things, but you can't control everything. I never known somebody as strong and full of moral courage, but if you don't start being realistic about your role on this here earth, I'm 'fraid Earl or Bean is gonna come in my kitchen one day and tell me you ate your gun. No man, or even God, could whip the special light out of your eyes, your soul. But if you don't get a hold on this thing, you gonna end up killing yourself."

No one likes the mirror held up to the front side of their soul. Nobody likes the fact someone can know you, what's deep down inside, so true. This old woman who had bandaged my cuts and scrapes, who had healed my body for the entirety of my life, was now looking so much deeper. She knew the part that was self-destructive. She saw it, no matter how hard I tried to hide it from the rest of the world.

There was a second there, lying on the floor, I hated her for it. I never wanted to let anyone in that deep. I had built a damned high wall around those feelings and the first one who put their head over it was bound to get it shot off. But a feeling scaled the wall, attempted escape, and before I could slap it back down like I'd been doing my whole life, she saw it, embraced it and took a picture which she now held in front of me.

She took the rag off of my head and dipped it into a pot of water, then

144

put it back. I grabbed her hand and looked deep into her eyes. She didn't move, but returned my look and said, "I know baby. I know."

***

The shop was still closed, the lights were off, and neither of the boys were there. I pushed through the front door. Earl and Bean were sitting on a pair of stumps under an oak tree. I walked over with my tail between my legs and sat on a bench swing. We stayed in silence for what seemed a very long time. I needed to say some things, but I was having trouble getting started.

An old bloodhound was curled around Earl's legs and he stroked the dog's floppy ears with a casual consistency. The dog got up with a lazy yawn, came over, and buried his nose in my crotch. I began to knead both of the long, velvety ears. "I'm sorry, Earl," I said, still looking into the dog's sad eyes.

"It's all right, Cloud. I know you didn't mean it."

This was worse. I wished he'd been mad, demanding a pound of flesh for my transgression. But that's not Earl. He's the sweet one between us. Always understanding of what the other might be suffering.

"They killed Cannery last night after we left and burnt the Site to the ground," I told them.

Both of them stared at me with a cringing feeling of shock and sadness. They'd the same relationship with her as myself over the years. Bean got to his feet and bellowed, "What... why the hell... who in the whole fucked up world?"

He kicked the stump, and a large gash marked his lack of understanding. Earl buried his face in his large calloused hands and began to cry. Bean continued around the yard taking his anger out on every inanimate object he could find.

We all wallowed in our own pity and lack of understanding. Bean grabbed an axe and began busting up a pile of wood. Earl continued to sob into his hands, and I sat there feeling bad for my role in Cannery's death, bad for beating up on Earl, and probably most of all for letting it get to me so badly, for letting even my best friends see how I felt. Misery was the one standing in the middle of the ring with hand held high, by a bitch of a referee who didn't seem to play fair.

I'd struggled for years with the concept of *fair*, trying to decide what merited the word. My current struggle only furthered my belief that simply because the world isn't a fair place, because everything is *not* fair, then we must change our view of the concept and accept all things in life as fair. It's a strange logic, I admit. But if you believe in making your own destiny, you really have no choice but to consider that *fair* is just about all the time.

I looked up to see Mama Bean coming toward us, carrying a large plate covered with a dishtowel. It had always been this way. Once she had mended our flesh with Band-Aids and alcohol, she mended our insides with a plate of chocolate chip cookies.

Chapter 42

I've known Earl and Bean since we were in first grade together. In that whole time, I don't remember ever seeing them apart. Some people said they were like one person, a mighty big person. Some others said they were queer, though never to their faces.

Earl is big and Bean is simply huge. I'd been mighty glad to have them on my team back when we were playing high school football. Earl is black, six-three or four, kind of round, hard muscle and fat. Bean is white, six-six, and all muscle.

They are devoted to each other as no brothers I've ever known, though you'd never know it by watching them give each other hell. But, many-the-time, I'd seen one or the other beat someone half to death over a redneck or nigger joke.

Bean's whole family died in a car accident when he was five years old. At the time he was known as Israel Quint Ladou. Earl's mom took him home from his family's funeral, and he's lived with them ever since. Earl's mom formally adopted him a year later and he took the last name of Bean as his own. Everyone I knew called him Bean ever since. Mrs. Bean had no husband, and she raised both of the boys as if they were brothers.

They still lived and worked in the same defunct old Florida motel, a crescent of nearly twenty cinder block rooms two miles outside of town. They hunted and fished, and, after the Army, took to taxidermy as a trade. They did it well and were always being sent exotic animals from all over the world to stuff or tan.

Earl's mother, Mama Bean, moved in with the boys after her house burned down a year or so ago. She cooked and cleaned the building and treated the boys like they were still ten years old. She was tough on them, but really I think she spoiled them rotten. She was the only living, breathing animal both boys were scared of.

Chapter 43

Phase Three – The Reckoning

Twelve men stood in the cinder block room. All of these men were vigilant in their belief of The Prophet and the Seekers' organization. Dressed in olive drab camouflage, their faces streaked with green, brown, and black markings, these were the men of Phase Three, responsible for delivering the death message the Prophet longed to inflict upon the world.

Daleen, flanked by the two Guardians, walked into the room. Always an imposing man, he took on a god-like aura. He strode to the center of the line of men and faced them, looking them over as a general would, preparing for battle. He was pleased with their conviction.

"Brothers, tonight we bring to light the meaning of our enterprise. We have suffered here in the bowels of this swamp, laboring to prepare ourselves in body, mind and especially spirit for the task at hand. The message we deliver this night will be heard around the world. It will have catastrophic economic and philosophical consequences. Tomorrow at this time we will surely find ourselves in the middle of a mighty battle, a war which will separate our beliefs from those of the common man. Everyone, and I do mean everyone, will see us as the enemy. And if we bare the truth, then let all of them be damned. I ask no less of you than your life, for what is a man's life but the sum of his beliefs? I expect no less of you than the last remaining gasp of breath you have on this earth. If any of you believe you are not up to the task at hand, stand forward and I will relieve you of this responsibility."

All the men stood where they were, ramrod straight and seething to deliver the message the Prophet professed.

"Each man here was chosen for his conviction and his belief in the cause we represent. When the patriots we call the founders of this country began a war of secession with the British government, many of them were labeled traitors. They were believed by some to be over-zealous and the very definition of terrorists. You will be so labeled. You will not earn your place in history in your lifetime. But, generations from now, your deeds will be compared to those of the same founding fathers."

The pre-game speech was powerful and the men stood aglow with pride. Their belief in the words of the Prophet was complete and unconditional.

Daleen produced a stack of note cards and passed one to each of the men. As each man accepted a card, the Prophet placed his hand upon his forehead and blessed them and their success in the mission. "Each of you will find on the card the name and location of a different farm or ranch within the local area. Tonight, you will take two other of our brother Seekers and visit these farms. You will seek out the largest bull at each location and make a sacrifice of the beast. You will then remove the bull's ears and tail and bring them back to Eden. Then we will prepare for the war which will surely follow. If our enemies discover you, you will eliminate them. If you are captured, you will make the final sacrifice of yourself and your team. No one will be taken prisoner. I will leave you to the Guardians who will make arrangements for the supplies you will need. Believe in me, and believe in God!"

With that, the Prophet left the room. One of the men, wearing his suit of war, wept.

Chapter 44

Blue has additional duties other than being a full-time agent for the Cable Department of Law Enforcement. She's also a member of the Cable Counties Rapid Response Team (RRT). This is a collection of the best and the brightest from each of the counties' Sheriff's departments as well as SWAT teams from each city police force. In the time I'd known Blue, she'd only been called out once to respond with the RRT when a gasoline tanker derailed one night in Marion County.

At four o'clock in the morning, the special beeper Blue keeps at all times came to life, filling the bedroom with an earsplitting shriek. By the time I was wiping the sleep from my eyes, I realized Blue was already suiting up, responding to radio commands and repeating a rapid-fire response of numbers and associated code.

Emma got dressed and headed for the kitchen. Sitting on the side of the bed, I was still trying to orient myself. I smelled coffee and heard noises coming from the kitchen. Blue saw me, her eyes met mine and conveyed a simultaneous sense of dread and excitement. She turned away and looked into the vanity mirror over the sink. She smoothed back her curly dark auburn hair and roughly tied it in place with a series of rubber bands. Blue is not a makeup person. She's one of those women who wake up looking fresh and beautiful under any circumstances. She threaded a long line of toothpaste onto a frayed brush that looked better suited to washing a toilet bowl, and brushed her teeth with a fury no person should wreak on their own mouth.

This was nothing new. Blue always brushed her teeth the way she did everything else—as if the fate of the world depended on her intensity. There was no lady-like grace. She quickly had toothpaste encircling the better part of her face. A long thick stalactite of Crest and spit dripped from her chin all the way to the porcelain sink. I could see the muscles in her forearm bulge, the veins of her arm protruding as if she were pumping life-giving air into a dead corpse instead of merely polishing her molars.

"What's up?" I asked with hope it was not what I thought.

The long stream of spit and toothpaste broke free and fell to the sink as she looked over at me. "It's the bulls, Cloud. I don't know exactly what happened, but it must be pretty big to call out RRT."

"Where?"

"I don't know the specific locations, but I can tell you it's multiple. Something is hitting the fan over all thirteen counties."

"I'm coming with you."

She spit again and said, "No, you are not! I already have one babysitter, Mac. I'm damn well not showing up at a crime scene with my boyfriend. You do what you need to do, call Mac, do what you do, but you do it apart from me." A raindrop of the Crest colored remnants of her efforts fell onto the front of her uniform. She turned back to the sink and splashed water over her face and made vulgar gurgling sounds as she rinsed.

She left and I stayed on the bed for a moment wondering why the hell am I only attracted to people, places, and events that are violent? Why does everything in my life revolve around struggle and torture? I stood up and looked into the mirror splashed with toothpaste drops. A ghost looked back at me and delivered the message through blazing eyes.

Live hard, be passionate, and don't accept anything less than absolute integrity.

I mumbled to myself, "Besides who the hell else could put up with you?"

In the kitchen, Emma was burning toast and pop tarts preparing a breakfast on the go in her unique Emma fashion—that poor quality in food could always be overcome by quantity.

I found Blue in the guest bedroom strapping a spare concealed Beretta to her vest. "Call me on the mobile when you get more details," I said.

"I'll do what I can, but you know they don't call us out on an RRT mission if it's not hot."

I walked over to where she was standing, one foot on the bed, strapping on another backup weapon. I grabbed her roughly, surprising her and myself with the passion dominating the room. The weapon, in its holster, slipped from her hand and fell to the floor. She looked at me wild-eyed, ready to hit me if she needed to. I put my hands on the sides of her face and looked long and deep into her eyes. "Blue, don't *prove* yourself to death. Emma and I love you. We won't be able to walk calmly among the rest of the people on this earth if you fuck up and don't come home one day."

At that moment, as if by some divine intervention from the gods of special effects, a huge roar of sentiment belted from the speakers wired into each room of the house. The sound was deafening. Emma was aware of the conflict, making her point with huge noise. The singer, Nina Simone, crushed the silence with her passionate wails about "Feeling Good."

Blue reached up and pulled my hands away. "And don't *you* protect me to death!" She kissed me deeply making me wonder for a moment if she knew this would be the last kiss we shared.

At the edge of the kitchen I saw Blue lock onto Emma's eyes. Electricity passed between them. Emma handed Blue a brown paper bag and a stainless steel thermos. Blue took them and walked to the door. Opening it, she stopped still facing the black night yet to erupt into morning. She never turned around but said, with what I'm sure were tears on her face, "I love you both." Then she went out, softly shutting the door.

"Go ahead and get ready. I'll put together something for you to eat on the go." Emma said in a worried motherly tone. She was concerned for Blue and wanted to make sure I was out there ready to slay any dragons which might come for her.

I did a quick locker room drill, showering, shaving and getting dressed for the big game. In the shower I began to think through what course I should take. I wanted to find out what was going on with the RRT and Blue and get there as quickly as possible. That was not what Blue wanted, and if I honestly thought about it, I was pretty secure in her abilities, as well as the abilities of the rest of the RRT.

She had said whatever was going on was at multiple locations all over the Cable Counties. I figured my best bet was Rufus Ford. I would head over to his ranch and see if death had followed this night. Rufus was a man of action and he would find out through the cattlemen's grapevine what had happened.

As I was heading out the door, Emma approached with another brown paper bag and a bottle of Gatorade. I reached for the bag, but instead Emma circled her arms around me and pulled me tight. "Look after her, Cloud, and yourself as well." I took the bag and the bottle and gave her a confident wink neither she nor I believed.

Chapter 45

I pulled the truck into the arc driveway at Rufus Ford's home. There was already a CDLE agent's cruiser parked in the drive. Rufus was standing in the yard drinking a cup of coffee and talking to Jim Turner, the squat agent who loved me so much. Both men stood silently watching as I got out of the truck and headed in their direction. Jake leapt from the cab behind me and began circling the yard, hunting the makers of ripe smells.

Jim Turner had the sour, scorned look of an animal defending his turf. "What're *you* doing here?"

I didn't bother even looking at him. "Rufus, what happened?"

"This thing has gone off the deep end. Whoever is doing this made one hell of a statement last night."

Jim Turner took a step towards me, putting a hand on Ford's arm. "This is a Cable Department of Law Enforcement matter. We don't need any *private talent*."

"Listen Jim, this thing is a lot bigger than we first thought. People who mean a great deal to me have been hurt and killed. I don't have any time to strut around and make feathered passes with any banty rooster."

Turner turned crimson. He should have reached for his radio to tell them an interloper was getting too close to a crime scene. But he was a small man and always had been a small man—the disease of the small man was coursing through his veins at a fatal rate. He reached for his gun, and I stepped in and popped him, two in the gut and one on the chin. I could practically hear the glass break. He wondered what had happened, and his eyes struggled to stay in the present. They then rolled back in his head and he fell in a heap on the dewy grass.

Rufus Ford didn't move, didn't blink. He put the coffee cup to his lips and blew shortly before taking a sip. "He won't be voting for you for mayor."

"I'm not running."

"They killed another bull, Cloud. And this time they left a message. A note was taped to the horn of the best bull I had left."

"You got the note?"

He handed a curled sheet of paper to me.

"The gods you worship are dead. They never were gods to begin with. You, the American masses, have brought your disposable mentality to every corner of the world. This is the beginning of the end. The food you have eaten for the last year was tainted and will begin to drive you into the madness you so richly deserve. We seek no payment. I am no common foe. I want the pounds of flesh you have stolen over the years. Seek me out and you shall find Armageddon."

"What do you think, Cloud?"

"I think I've about had it with this game of slap and tickle with these mother fuckers."

It was barely six in the morning, but the farm was coming to life. Several trucks had pulled up to a corral and men in the fenced area saddled horses. A young girl ran from the house holding a cordless phone in her hand. She breathlessly stumbled forward. "Pappy, Pappy—phone, phone."

Rufus took the phone and girl up into his arms with one swoop. The girl showed pride in having delivered a very important message. Ford held the phone to his ear. "Ford."

His countenance didn't change, but I could tell from past dealings a storm was brewing. He squatted down and let the girl put her bare feet into the wet grass. She sat on his thigh and swung her tiny toes. After nearly a minute, Ford said, "I'll be here, and Cloud is with me." He clicked the phone dead and handed it back to the little girl, and said with a light pat of her fanny, "Take this back in to your Grandma."

She ran back into the house with the same speed she had on the way out, the phone raised above her head. "Grandma, Grandma—phone, phone."

"That was Tom Goodrich. He's on his way over here. Eleven other bulls were killed over all thirteen counties last night, and each one had the same note taped to them. Some CDLE agents caught up with a Hummer heading off one of the farms up in the north end of Cable. They had a shootout. One agent is dead and one is missing."

I felt my heart tighten and a large swallow of something evil fell toward my stomach. "Who were the agents?"

"He didn't know."

I ran back to my truck and yanked the phone from the cradle, pressing the speed dial for Blue's mobile number. The phone rang and rang and rang. Jake was sitting in front of me looking solemn and expectant. After five rings the recorded message from Blue's phone kicked in. I put the phone back in its cradle.

***

I thought for a moment and then grabbed the phone again. I filed through the stored numbers and found Knox's mobile number. After one ring he picked up.

"Mac Knox."

"It's Cloud." I said with as much tolerance as I could muster.

"I'm gonna tell you this Cloud, and I expect you to act right."

I slipped to a sitting position in the doorway of the truck.

"Blue and Agent Dix went to Ben McCullers' ranch as a part of the Rapid Response Team. We had a call out from a farm over in Levy County and we sent every agent we have to a different farm. All farms reported dead bulls, except at McCullers place, there were no other bulls there. Evidently the perps were still searching for one when Blue and Dix came up on them. There was a shootout, Dix is dead, and Cloud, I'm just as sorry as I can be, but they took Blue. We're assuming since they took her she's still alive."

I sucked it up, the way I had been sucking it up my entire life. Every important person in my life had abandoned me through death. I would not let this happen again. I could hear Knox calling to me, "Cloud? Cloud, are you there?"

I broke the connection and looked for a moment at Jake. He seemed to know somehow the desperate nature of the situation. If I had said to him, "Go and attack the vicious beast killing Blue," he would have flung the entirety of his twenty pounds at the fire-breathing menace.

Rufus Ford read the signs on my face. He threw the coffee mug at a tree supporting one end of a slinking hammock. The cup shattered. "Boy, are you ready to commit? Ready to do the right thing?"

I stood from my position of defeat and looked at this hardened, rough man. "I'm getting ready to kill some people, old man. If you have some support to offer, I'll take it. If you're still trying to teach me what a bastard I am because you're still pissed about Daisy, then get ready 'cause I'm gonna stomp your ass first."

"Good, that's very good. I may not have to resent you for the rest of your life. Every one of those men you see in the corral over there are Texas bounty hunters I hired about a week ago. They're ready to bring in the beast, they just need a sheriff to lead their posse. I'm coming along, but I'll let you lead the way."

"They got Blue."

"I figured. So now you got something to lose. Cloud, for the whole of the time I've known you, I thought you were a spectator. You've been a winner. Winning is easy for you. Too easy. Made you cocky, detached—like a steer trying to tell a bull what to do. This time your heart is latched onto someone else. Her life is at stake. You think you been tested before? This one's for all the marbles."

"Get those bounty hunters and their horses loaded up on one of those sixteen wheelers. I'm going to make a few arrangements, then we're going to the Scrub. That's where the bastards are. Rufus, if you come with us, well, that may be the end. I'm coming out of that swamp with a whole lot of bodies. I expect most of them won't be breathing. But if Blue is in there, then everybody who took her or hurt her is going to be in a bag."

"I'm a gray man with six daughters and no male heir. If you measure up to what you're saying, I'd be right proud to put it all on the line with you."

Chapter 46

I placed a call through to Earl and Bean. "They got Blue and I have a general idea where they're holding her. Rufus Ford has a bunch of men, bounty hunters, and we're going to the Scrub to get Blue and put an end to this mess."

Earl was on the other end of the phone and I could hear him exhale painfully. "Bean and I'll be ready in ten minutes, whatcha want us to do?"

"Load up your weapons, bring the bow and arrows, as well as your Jon Boat, I think we may need them. I'll call you back in thirty minutes to tell you where to meet us."

Agent Jim Turner was coming back to land of the living. He shook his head, then wiped himself off before hurrying to his squad car, where he sent duel rooster tails of dirt in the air with his retreat.

Just as I was putting the phone into the cradle I saw Tom Goodrich arrive. He and Rufus Ford went into a small office to the side of the main corral. I followed fast and banged the door open. Goodrich was standing in the middle of the room, his head hung, and Rufus was sitting in the big leather swivel chair behind his desk.

"Cloud, I'm just as sorry as I can be about Blue," Goodrich said.

"Tom, what do you know so far about this whole scene?"

Goodrich looked over to Rufus Ford, who widened his eyes and said, "Tell him for Christ sakes!"

"Mac Knox has called in the federal authorities—the FBI, the USDA. The letters taped to the bulls make us think whoever is behind this has more on his mind than just killing bulls. The Federal people are already on their way, several agents flew out of Atlanta within an hour of his call. It seems the Center for Disease Control in Atlanta received an anonymous tip saying some of the very same things in the letters we got off our dead bulls. The tip-off sent to the CDC went a little further, saying a disease of huge proportion has been introduced to several herds in the southeast over the last year. It's Mad Cow — holy shit, Mad Cow Disease. They say the virus has had enough time to mature and practically every beef and dairy cow in the United States is now at risk. Thank God the Feds and the CDC have been planning for a situation just like ours. They're bringing their whole containment operation as well as some investigators down. They should all be here by noon."

Goodrich took a breath and asked, "What have you found out so far?"

"All along I've been telling anybody who would listen this was more than what it seemed. I don't know anything about Mad Cow disease. I don't know anything about something that would affect the whole United States. What I do know is some group, a cult of some kind, is responsible. They're holed up somewhere in the Scrub, which is a mighty big area. They call themselves the Seekers and I saw the prick in charge one night over at The Construction Site before it burnt down and Cannery Row was killed. They were using The Construction Site as a distribution site for drugs, mostly to the college crowd and the local farm hands. I thought early on that *this* was their whole operation, drugs. But now it seems they had something else in mind all along and maybe were financing their real operation with drug money."

"Do you think it's somebody from around here, somebody local?" Rufus Ford said.

"They're not local, at least not the people in charge. I think they've recruited some of the local troublemakers, but that was just to get a few more soldiers in their army. I called it a cult earlier, because I think they have some fundamentalist views. The majority of the group thinks they're doing God's bidding, like some modern-day Jim Jones, Guiana tragedy, in the making."

Ford looked at me with cold intent. "What do you think we should do?"

"Well, we're not going to wait for the Feds. We're not going to let this turn into some Waco stand-off with Blue in the middle being bartered for as hostage bait. I already told you, I'm going into the Scrub to find them. I hope you'll send your merry band of bounty hunters with me. I already talked to Earl and Bean."

Goodrich looked doubtful and shook his head. "I don't think that's such a wise move. We should wait for the Federal people to get here and take control of the situation."

"Tom, you want to make sure the fatted calves of the Cable Counties get sold. You want to make sure all of the cattlemen keep sending their annual dues into your organization and keep paying your salary. I want Blue back. I want to find out who killed Cannery Row, Billy, my dog, *and* who took Mildred. And I tell you something else, I would kill every goddamn bull, steer, and cow in the whole world myself to make sure those things happen."

Goodrich looked to Ford for support, but he was already standing and putting on a leather pistol belt he'd gathered from the bottom drawer of his desk.

"Cloud," Goodrich said, "remember you work for me. You work for the best interest of the Cattlemen's Association."

I gritted my teeth. "Listen hard, windshield cowboy. First of all, Ben McCullers asked me for a favor. Like I told you that first day at the diner, I work for myself. And if you tried to stop me once I got started, you would become the enemy."

"I can tell you one thing, Cloud. The Cattlemen's Association will not pay for you to go out and make this situation worse by practicing some form of vigilante justice."

I stepped towards Goodrich and grabbed the red handkerchief he wore around his neck to make sure people thought of him as an authentic cowboy. "Bull…*shit!*" I said, and turned to Rufus Ford. "I'll meet you in one hour where Mildred's store used to be. Have your men ready. We're going into that swamp to get Blue back."

Chapter 47

Back at Eden, the last of the Hummers pulled into the compound. Daleen was sitting in a rocking chair on the dirt porch of the Quonset hut, which served as meeting hall and church. Three men got out of the Hummer and stood giving each other high fives. They became aware of the Prophet's gaze and quickly ended their celebration, coming respectfully over to the porch. They could hardly contain their excitement on having brought back not a mere pair of bull's ears and a tail—but a real live law officer.

Daleen stood and rose to his full height. "Was your mission successful, brother Seekers?"

The leader announced, "Sir, we found no bull at that particular farm, but during our search we were engaged by the enemy. They must have been notified due to the success of our brothers at other farms. We engaged the enemy in a firefight, and I am proud to say we killed one of them at the site. We were fortunate enough to capture the other cop and have her bound and gagged in the back of the vehicle."

They waited for the inevitable praise to follow. Daleen looked at them with a far-away disbelief. The storm began to whip his adrenalin into a fury. "Brothers, I was certain my instructions were clear. You were to kill the enemy, if engaged. *Kill* the enemy, not capture, and most definitely not bring anyone back to Eden."

The men's broken pride fell to the ground like so much dirty moss from an oak. The voice of the leader of the small group took on a pleading nature.

"But sir, my Prophet, we thought she would be a far greater weapon with which we could fight our enemy if we held her here as a hostage."

The voice of the Prophet remained calm, but his eyes clouded with a violence the men had never witnessed. "Her? Are you telling me your hostage is a woman?"

They went to the Hummer and the leader pulled back a tarp. On the floor of the vehicle lay the bruised and bloodied form of Blue, dressed in all RRT black. She was awake, her bright blue-green eyes fluttering as they adjusted to the light. There was no fear in the eyes, only a rage making her look more like a wild animal.

"Why is she so beaten?"

"She struggled, she fought unnaturally for such a small woman. It took all three of us to subdue her. She cursed us and you—she cursed God."

Daleen yanked the bandana from Blue's mouth. She said nothing. No verbal tirade, no threats, no pleading. Daleen's mouth bent into a reptilian smile. "She might be valuable at that. What's your name?"

Nothing. The cop lay still in the cargo area looking back into the eyes of the Prophet with the same quiet hate.

"Ah, a strong one. Good, it has been some time since I have practiced my interrogation techniques. Bring her to my office. And brothers, let there be no mistake. Even if she turns out to be of some benefit, under other circumstances, I would kill all three of you for disobeying my orders."

The men were aware of the Prophet's power. They tried to make up for their mistake by zealously carrying out his commands. They threw the tarp on the ground and slammed Blue down, using it as a litter to hurry her into the cinderblock, dank room that served as the Prophet's office.

Daleen sat behind his desk. "Leave us. Go and prepare for battle."

They hurried out, glad to have escaped the Prophet's wrath. Daleen slid from behind the desk and got a firm grip on the thick red hair and pulled Blue into a sitting position. She never winced, never pulled back or fought. Her eyes never left those of the man whose hand was now tethered to her hair.

"I will not unbind your hands or feet as a safety precaution. It's a precaution I take on your behalf, so you should be thankful. If I were to cut you free and you were to fight me, I would surely have to kill you. But, killing you is not what I want, at least not yet. Time is short and what I want is information. I want to know the strength of your Sheriff's department. I want to know what they know about me and my Seekers. I want to know what plan they have formulated to combat us. You will give me this information or I will make your death so slow and excruciating, you will wish for hell's fury just to make life here on earth end.

Daleen let go of her hair and sat on the edge of his desk. "Tell me what I want to know."

Blue looked at him, and for the first time in many years, surprise struck Daleen's face when she smiled.

Chapter 48

I drove back to the house as fast as the diesel would go. As I was coming to a stop, I saw Emma shutting the front door of our home, her face was cautious and concerned. No matter how difficult this situation became, I couldn't imagine anything being harder than what I was getting ready to do. I gathered my emotions and dread into a tight ball and mentally stuck it in my back pocket.

I met her at the end of the brick walk she and Blue had built. The house and the walk lay under a huge canopy of live oaks. The plants bordering the walk are the variety that grow best sheltered from direct sunlight. Large green ferns, caladiums in dark hues of green and pink, and enormous elephant ears all dripped with the morning dew. The hand-made jungle engulfed her and seemed to make her smaller than she really was. With each step she took toward me, I could feel the anxiety build.

Jake sensed the heaviness of the moment and had forgone his usual "balls out" exploration of the yard to escort me. I met her eyes and walked quickly until I was a foot in front of her. I reached out and took her hands in mine. "They have Blue. They've taken her, and I am going to get her back."

She stumbled for a moment, swaying and her knees gave way. I caught her and helped Emma sit down on an upturned plastic bucket. She put her head between her knees, trying to catch her breath and stop the retch in her throat. I held her head against my waist and brushed dark blue-black hair with my hand. After a few minutes, she stood up and looked at me.

"Are you sure she's alive?"

I'd prepared myself for the question. I was unsure myself, but deep in my soul I knew she had to be. "Yes, she's still alive. I'm going to get her, but I need your help."

In a strange way this seemed to comfort her. Emma isn't the kind to sit by and let things unravel as they may. She needs to be exerting some kind of effort. "What do you need me to do?"

"Let's go inside and I'll tell you."

Emma called the University, saying she had a family emergency. In the kitchen, we perched on bar stools around a wooden butcher block. I pushed a glass of water towards her and she drained the entire glass. Sometimes you just have to have even the smallest physiological task to keep your mind focused.

I told her, "Everything I've been working on seems to be a front. The bulls being killed was the least of it. The burning of The Construction Site was just housekeeping. Jack and Billy were casualties of war. These people have been systematically infecting the herds of the largest farms in the Cable Counties with Mad Cow disease. It's also contagious to humans. With the distribution of beef cattle to states like Texas and Oklahoma over the last few years, this may have become a national emergency. If that's the case, then everyone who's eaten a Whopper or a Big Mac in the past year is in danger of contamination."

Emma's eyes grew wide, but she remained the ready listener.

"Mac called in the FBI, USDA, and the Center for Disease Control. I imagine they're already on the ground and will be swarming Ben McCullers' ranch within the hour. The Feds will see Blue as an acceptable casualty. They'll take a week to try and sort things out and negotiate with the bastards for some kind of information to help them contain the disease. Even with the Governor's backing, Mac might try and fight them at first, but I'm sure he'll become a spectator or support at most, very quickly. Our priority is Blue. I don't give a damn what happens if we can't get her back. So we'll be fighting against time, the good guys, *and* the bad guys. I need for you to take care of the *good* guys, just for a few hours."

"What are you going to do?"

"Rufus Ford has some able men. Earl, Bean and I, along with Ford's people are going into the Scrub. We're going to find the motherfuckers, burn their houses down, and bring Blue back."

"Cloud, you know I believe in you more than any man alive. But you always think you can just walk into any situation and break somebody's face or burn their house down and fix the situation. I'm not risking Blue's life on that. Are you sure you can get her? How many men are helping you?"

"You know I wouldn't risk Blue's life. This is the only way. If we wait for the Feds to get involved, the well-intentioned bureaucracy will kill her just as surely as those bastards down in the Scrub."

Her eyes swept the kitchen and lingered on several pictures of our little family. The refrigerator was covered with magnetic photo holders of the happiest moments of our lives. Emma pulled a gerbera daisy from a vase sitting in the center of the butcher block. "Blue cut this flower yesterday. She and I brought a whole bucket full of them in and made arrangements. I love you with all my heart, but you understand Blue is the center of the universe as far as I'm concerned."

I nodded. "So we're in agreement about that. Will you do what I need you to do?"

She looked at me for a long time, measuring my intent. Satisfied at last, she asked, "What do you want me to do?"

I took ten minutes to outline my plan and to explain her role. When I was done, I asked if she understood, but she was already moving toward the bedroom. Moments later she reappeared wearing jeans and a light flannel top. She took my face with both dark tanned hands. "You go get our girl. You bring my Blue back to me."

I went into the spare bedroom. In a walk-in closet, behind the clothes Emma and Blue no longer wore, was my personal arsenal. I pulled a trunk from under the shoe rack and began filling a black canvass bag with everything I'd need. Only minutes later, I was back in my truck and driving to the landing strip.

The morning haze drifted over its surface. I punched a garage door opener clipped to my sun visor and the doors to the hanger where I keep the

Beechcraft twin engine began to roll upward. I unloaded the supplies and the weapons from the truck and reloaded them into the plane. The whole affair took maybe fifteen minutes. I taxied the Beechcraft to the beginning of the runway and sat revving the plane, building RPM's for takeoff. By habit, my hand picked up the radio handset and I almost asked for permission from the local air traffic control tower for a little airspace. With faint regret, I put the handset back in its rack.

I gently rubbed the fake leather dashboard. "Thank you, old girl for so many safe flights. I'll miss you." If everything went as planned, I was sure my beautiful plane would never land in this pasture again. For that matter, I might not either.

Chapter 49

A solid iron hook was set into the cinder block wall about seven feet off the floor. Daleen felt all of the hate he'd harbored for so long for this government and these *people* form into a single nucleus. He jumped from behind the desk and grabbed Blue, snatching her upright and nearly lifting her off the ground to slip the cable ties binding her hands over the iron hook. She was fairly dangling, just able to support her weight by standing on the very points of her toes. The ties cut into her wrists and the green-black bruises around her wrists began to redden with blood.

He thrust his hand, snake-like under the bulletproof vest she still wore, fumbling at her breast pockets, roughly massaging the ample flesh below the fabric. He never let his eyes leave hers. She drilled back with her own unflinching gaze. His breath bathed her face. It was sweet, not in a candy or pleasant aroma, but as if he had recently eaten raw bloody meat. He found the small black badge case in her pocket and grinned.

Daleen flipped it open and saw the silver badge of a Cable Department of Law Enforcement Agent. He then extracted a small white hard Agent I.D. card bordered with deep forest green and gold lines. He read aloud, "Agent Sarah Tableau, expert qualification in firearms and tactical reconnaissance. Member of the Rapid Response Team. Medals for bravery in the site of eminent danger, valor, and a mortal wound." He snapped the case shut and threw it on his desk. "Well, well, Agent Tableau you *are* a real life hero, a true expert in the methods of your government's fanatical law enforcement. What have they taught you about true warfare? Very little, I imagine. Your government depends on the "bigger gun" theory of crushing its enemies."

Blue remained in permanent lockjaw.

"Since you will never be leaving Eden—that's what we call our little slice of heaven here—I guess I should tell you something about myself. It may motivate you to speak. My name is Bent Daleen and the followers here call me the Prophet. In reality, I'm an international terrorist. I've worked in countless countries over the past twenty years, and, as you can see, I've never been caught. Actually, I've never even been in jeopardy of being apprehended. I've killed so many people, all who deserved it, I can't even begin to count or remember them all. I am a holy warrior. I am the sanctified living *will* of the one true God."

He slapped her three times.

"I hope you do not doubt my resolve. It would be the very last mistake you ever make. I need to know what your sheriff is planning."

Blue pursed her lips together, made a loud hawking sound, and spit a blood-slimed gob into his face. It stuck and he made no effort to wipe it away. She grinned malevolently at him.

Daleen pulled a large serrated knife from a sheath. He held it up to her face and let the tip rest at the edge of her right eyelid.

"Did you know women who commit suicide very rarely do damage to their own face? They choose, even in death, to embrace vanity. I suppose they feel their friends and loved ones will feel more despair if they can still view the intact face of a lovely corpse. Furthermore, did you know when an angry domestic situation arises the man will, more times than not, do damage to the woman's face first? It seems to get their attention very quickly."

Blue gathered her lips again to deliver the same insult. Daleen slapped her three quick times again. Blood began to drool from the corner of her mouth. He pressed the knife to the same spot and asked, "What does the sheriff intend to do?"

Her steel gaze remained.

Daleen raked the back end of the blade from the corner of her eye down the entire length of her freckled cheek. This got a response. Blue shrieked a blood-curdling scream. When the scream subsided, her eyes came back with a renewed intensity.

"I see you are of a sturdier lot. But I am an expert. Rest assured, you will tell me what I want to know. The human body can only take so much pain and humiliation."

Daleen cut away the bulletproof vest. It fell to the floor in a blood-streaked heap. Then he slashed the front of her uniform open and made rags of the black material. Blue wore a gray undershirt with "Attitude" written on it. He bent his mouth into an appraising look. "That seems quite accurate."

Daleen went back to his desk and removed the silver star from the black case, dropping it into the cradle of a burning candle. Daleen turned his head quickly to catch the eyes of Blue watching his every move. He snickered to himself.

The Prophet did a small pirouette to return in front of Blue. He was truly enjoying himself more than he could remember. He grabbed the collar of her undershirt and deftly slid the knife from top to bottom exposing a red jog bra. He looked at her, bemused, and snipped the narrow belt of silk fabric between her breasts. She hung against the concrete wall, exposed.

"Do law officers wear their badges on the left or right? Still no answer? I guess it really doesn't matter. I will choose the left." He bent his head to her left breast and licked a small brown nipple, anxiously protruding.

A convulsing sense of nausea overcame Blue, and she opened her mouth to vomit. Nothing came out, but a glistening silver strand of spit and a high moan. Daleen pulled on a leather glove and took the smoldering badge from the cradle, holding it in front of her eyes. "Do you have anything you now wish to tell me? No? Then we will make you the first agent in the Cable Counties to have a permanent badge of honor."

Daleen pressed the silver star to Blue's naked left breast. She seized, her head jerking back hard against the concrete wall. He gritted his teeth and put his full body weight behind the effort, branding the star into her skin. She writhed and kicked her bound feet against the unyielding wall. He leaned his snarling face close to her breast and inhaled deeply the pungent odor of burning flesh.

Chapter 50

A loud banging rattled the door. Daleen never let up the pressure on the silver star, bellowing over his shoulder, "Do *not* disturb me."

Two voices pleaded from outside. The Prophet hardly noticed—he was in his element. Blue convulsed one last time, then fainted. As her head drooped towards her chest, he caught one last glimpse of the fire in her eyes. He savored the pain behind the eyes for as long as the embers glowed.

The banging was fierce now, the voices stretched in panic. He dropped the star to the bloody wet cement floor and strode to the door. The anxious faces of the two Guardians greeted him.

"We need you. The enemy is at hand."

Daleen looked back at Blue, hanging lifeless on the iron hook. He gave a satisfied smirk and followed the Guardians.

Chapter 51

I was flying near the edge of the Scrub—a backward-assed, country version of the Bermuda Triangle. I got a visual on the barren black-top of County Road 345. I couldn't see any traffic for miles in either direction. I throttled back and lined up the Beechcraft with the dotted yellow line running down the center of the road. Crop dusters land their planes on country roads all the time, but I'd never done it. I had, however, landed in worse conditions in jungles and deserts in other countries. There was really no time to think about it.

Five minutes later, the plane was on the ground, I taxied to the burnt out hulk of Mildred's store.

There was a sixteen-wheel cattle hauler already there. The men I had seen before at Rufus Ford's corral were unloading a series of very large, muscled horses. Rufus was standing at the rear of his pickup talking to Earl and Bean. Everyone was watching the plane, surprised.

I unloaded the photographs I'd taken from the air earlier and a yellow legal pad. I thanked the men for being there. They all looked at me as if to say, "Where else would we be at a time like this?" I spread the photos on the tailgate of Ford's truck and put a little rock on each one of them to hold against the wind. The sky was turning dark and it looked like it would be a day of unrelenting rain, suffocating heat and humidity.

Rufus Ford was the first to speak. "What in the hell are you planning here, Cloud?"

"We're going to hit them fast and from every direction. I don't know exactly how many of them there are, but there must be quite a few to kill all of those bulls last night. We're going in by air, land, and sea so to speak. Hopefully the surprise of seeing us come from so many directions will give the illusion there are too many of us to fight and they will just lay down their weapons and surrender. But on a more realistic note, when they hunker down and start firing back I want to make sure we can't be outflanked or out-maneuvered. We won't have all of our eggs in remotely the same basket."

The seriousness of the situation became apparent on the faces of the men. The adrenaline and passion had been flowing so strong nobody thought we would do anything but just go in through the front gate with guns blazing. My days at West Point, and later more exclusive and shadowy schools, studying assault and warfare, were once again coming in handy.

I took my time explaining the photos and getting everyone familiar with the lay of the swamp. I thought it supremely important everyone be very clear on the timing of the mission. Then I showed them a map and used a florescent highlighter and black grease pencil to mark certain critical points. The men were all quick studies, and I felt they clearly had a grasp of the locations we would hit.

"Here's how it will go down. Earl and Bean will put their Jon Boat in here at the fish camp. We'll give them a head start because I think it'll take a little time to get around in the swamp. Rufus, you and your men will ride in by horseback. You'll come in through the front gate."

Earl looked up from the map beginning to understand the multifaceted assault. He scratched his bald head and looked at me. "What are *you* going to do?"

"I'm going to bring the plane in low and pretty fast. Right about here," I pointed to a long stretch of dirt road. "I'm going to try and land. Hopefully I'll draw all of their attention and give you guys a chance to get in close before they know what hit them."

Earl looked skeptical. "Doesn't seem like enough of a runway to set that thing down."

"It's enough. Besides, if I come up a little short, I intend to use this

Quonset hut as emergency brakes." I tapped the map.

"It sounds like you're saying you're going to crash your plane into the center of their compound and hope you come out alive," Earl said.

I summoned all of my remaining patience. "I'm doing a little more than hoping. Blue is in that compound somewhere. I don't know exactly where, so I won't be risking running into any building where I think they might be keeping her."

Earl was shaking his head. Bean quickly picked up on this and began swinging his large domed head in exactly the same metronomic cadence. Earl said, "I don't know, Cloud. There doesn't seem to be any reason to go in there... all Kamikaze and shit."

"Damn it, Earl, we don't have time to talk about alternative plans. I'm telling you, this is what we're going to do."

Chapter 52

Emma drove her red Ford Explorer into the yard of Ben McCullers' place. The Federal guys had made good time. There was a series of large, white, very studious looking recreational vehicles parked around the house and barn. Cloud had asked that she be mildly hysterical when she arrived here. On any other day this would've required substantial acting skills.

Knox ran into the yard waving his hands trying to get her to stop. It was exactly the reaction Cloud and Emma were hoping for. Emma locked the brakes and came to a skidding halt. She jumped out, leaving the motor running, and dashed straight into Knox's arms.

"Whoa there, woman. Calm down. Where do you think you're going?"

Emma went into her lines. "Where's Blue? Is she all right? What's going on? What are all these RVs doing here?"

Knox grabbed her by the shoulders and shook her. "Emma, hey, get a grip on things. Calm down. What're you doing here?"

Tears were coming down her cheeks in great torrents. They weren't manufactured for his inspection. "Mac, tell me straight, what's going on? Is Blue all right?"

He shook her again, maybe a little harder than he had to. "Hey, listen, Blue is going to be okay. We're doing everything we can. The FBI is here along with some people from the Center for Disease Control. They've taken over the investigation. They're good people—people who know what they're doing."

Emma needed the comforting. She was following Cloud's plan, but she was also human and needed a strong shoulder. "Mac, Blue is very important to me. I couldn't bear it if she was hurt. What's going on?"

He pulled her to his chest and hugged her with sincere affection. Even a man as hardened as Knox couldn't stand to see his friend in so much pain. "Shh, quiet now, everything is going to be all right." She squeezed him tight and hung onto the rock she knew would always be there for her.

Chapter 53

The plan had been for Emma to find out what was going on at the McCullers' ranch and to call me as soon as she could. She was also supposed to delay Knox for about an hour from trying to find out what I was doing. Then she was to tell him everything—tell him me and a group of men were going into the Scrub to lay siege on the compound. I had given her a map of the area where I thought the Seekers were holed up and some aerial photographs I'd taken to corroborate my theory.

Emma started out strong, but the emotional threat to her, because of the physical threat to her family, was too much. She broke down early and told Knox what I was up to.

When she called me, her tone was apologetic. "I tried, Cloud, but I was just too worried about you and Blue. I told Mac everything. He's standing right here and he wants to talk to you."

Earl and Bean had left about thirty minutes before, Rufus Ford and his rough riders twenty minutes earlier. This wasn't the head-start I'd hoped for, but it was probably enough. Knox's booming voice came over the phone as I sat in my plane preparing for takeoff.

"I don't know what the hell you're planning here, but don't. Let these fellas from the FBI sort through things and make a plan with calmer heads at the wheel."

"Sorry buddy, you know I can't do that. Those guys will be well-meaning, but by the time they figure out what to do, Blue might be dead."

"Boy, you know I care about Blue just about as much as you, so don't patronize me. At least wait for me to get there so we can go in together."

"That would be impossible. Everyone else is already on their way. I'm the last to get started. Just listen to what I told Emma to tell you and come on to the Scrub as fast as you can."

"You're a stubborn, hard-headed son of a bitch. I just hope you don't end up making this situation a lot worse for all of us, both legally and personally."

"I hope I know what I'm doing, too." I clicked the phone dead and revved up the twin engines for takeoff.

***

I wanted to make a pass over the compound to make sure everything was just the way I thought it should be, but the plane would warn them. They were already preparing for something big and letting them know *big* was coming would only hurt our chances. This meant I was going in nearly blind. I'd have to rely on the photographs I took earlier. That was going to be tricky.

I'd told Earl, Bean, and Rufus most of my plan. I'd noticed in one of my earlier photographs a building to the side of the big Quonset hut. It was really just a large pavilion with tall intermittent columns made of stacked cinder block covered with a tin roof. There were really no walls to speak of. This was really the building I intended to use as my emergency brakes, and I wasn't even going to try and land the plane in one piece, I was going to crash it into the building on purpose. I bled the fuel tanks down to a level I thought would give me just enough time to escape before the plane blew up. If the crash didn't ignite the plane, I intended to throw my lighter into the mix as soon as I was clear.

If I survived the landing.

Chapter 54

Bent Daleen stood in front of his army of almost sixty men, all trained by him. They were competent, if not expert. The most vital element Daleen possessed to carry out his master plan was these men's willingness to die. They believed so fervently in the message of the Prophet they were prepared, if not intent on, proving their devotion by making the ultimate sacrifice.

"Brothers, Seekers, the time is at hand. It is time to show the infidels who oppose us, to show the entire world the passion with which we hold our sacred beliefs. I am the Prophet, and I have been sent to make the world see its true self. You are the soldiers who will help me deliver that message this day. We will surely not all survive, but God has a place at his right hand for the blessed Seekers. If your brother falls, do not linger over his body. Push forward. Fight for what we believe, fight for me, fight onward for God."

With that, Bent Daleen began to give assignments to the Seekers. He positioned them expertly in every covered position within the compound, creating a very tight perimeter. The few women and children who lived in Eden had been sent away. He hadn't done this out of honor or chivalry. He simply knew men would not put their hearts into a fight if they were worrying about saving the women and children.

There was one thing Bent Daleen, the Prophet, knew that no one else at the compound did. No matter what, only one man would walk from the ashes of Eden at day's end. He intended to put up a terrific battle, but when it was all done, if any of the Seekers survived, Daleen would kill them himself.

Martyrs were the stuff headlines were made of in this self-indulgent country.

He wanted martyrs. He reflected on the tattoo of a dead enemy many years before. "Kill 'em all. Let God sort 'em out." He thought this a very accurate assessment of the facts.

Chapter 55

Lightning crackled in the sky. Some people called it heat lightening. It usually preceded a downpour of driving rain punctuated by even more intense lightning and thunder. I never flew under such conditions—unless my favorite person in the whole world was in eminent danger of being killed by a twisted zealot.

The bird's eye view from the plane allowed me to see Earl and Bean docking their Jon Boat at a swampy landing to the east of the compound. I could also just make out Rufus Ford and his rough riders pounding a trail.

The plane was revved to its maximum RPMs. This was the moment of no turning back—the moment of reckless abandon. I pulled the flaps back and kept the throttle rammed as high as it would go. The plane fought me; this was not the normal condition when flying this close to the ground. The heat vapors rose from the baked swamp and made it very difficult to control the lift of the Beechcraft. The entire cabin vibrated, and she seemed to question my loyalty.

I guided the plane into a pattern parallel to the tree-canopied dirt road leading to the compound. With a half mile to go, I eased the yoke forward and dropped to below three hundred feet, still in a shallow dive. Driving rain pelted the grinding plane. At fifty feet, I leveled off. I could see the buildings dotting the compound's geography. Tall pines brushed the wings. At this rate, I'd probably lose one to a knotted old evergreen, before crashing.

The first shots began punching into the hull of the plane. A bullet cracked the front windshield and spider webs spread. The shattering glass would send razor sharp shards hurtling through the cabin in seconds.

I picked out the building that would be my emergency brakes and set a due course. By now the plane was just ten feet from the ground. A hail of bullets rained in and around the cockpit. I expected one to tear through me at any moment. I felt the landing gear touch the ground only to be torn free under the furious speed and decent. I mentally counted backwards to the point of impact, yanking the throttle back, the plane skidded wildly along the ground. Men were running out of the way, firing their weapons over their shoulders.

One camouflaged loyalist slipped over and I felt the plane grind his corpse into the rough, rock-covered road. My aim had been true and the Beechcraft came to an abrupt stop in the clenched fist of the pavilion. I was thrown forward, smashing through the windshield. I kept my eyes open the whole time, seeing everything pass beside and even *through* me. I slid along a long concrete floor, cradling my body against itself, my arms over my face. A moment later, I surged into some bales of hay, knocking the wind from my lungs. I turned onto my back and gasped for air which wouldn't come.

The Beechcraft exploded, a terrific blast which took the roof off the pavilion. Bits of wood and tin swooped into the air in an infernal dance and rained back down on everything.

Fire swept from the dying plane quickly. A steady stream of what looked like burning lava flowed across the floor towards me. I gathered my feet and leapt into a stand of palmetto bushes. They weren't nearly as soft as the hay, the spines tearing at my arms, legs, and face.

From where I lay in the palmettos, I could see an incredible firefight. The Seekers *had* been justly distracted by the crashing plane and now a dozen men on horseback rode through the compound, firing every manner of gun and assorted military hardware from the backs of their dragon-like steeds. I glimpsed a huge hulk of a man that could only be Bean raise two of the fundamentalist bastards in unison above his head, each throat clutched in the bear-like vise grip of his hands. Bean slammed their faces together, cracking the bloody features of one against the other. One was Agent Jim Turner. Just as quickly, he discarded the limp bodies and went in search of his next victims.

I had these few seconds of lying in shock, watching Armageddon, to get my strength back. I was just about to roll onto my feet when a mammoth hand gripped my entire face and twisted my head around.

My eyes met a metallic-looking grin. It was the man I'd seen at The Construction Site—the man who vanished behind the green door. The devil behind the whole sorry mess. He slapped me twice back-handed to make sure I was awake and he would see the pain he wanted to inflict. This was the monster. *He meant for this to happen.* He was the only soul on the planet who was actually enjoying this moment. He bellowed against the continuing explosions and gunfire.

"I am Bent Daleen, the Prophet of Eden, and you must be the Anti-Christ I have been seeking my whole life?"

I understood this was not a statement; there was a question mark at the end of his sentence. He *wanted* to believe I was the Anti-Christ. He wanted to believe his was a holy war and he was moments from doing *the* God's bidding. I wouldn't give him the satisfaction.

I looked into those black eyes and said, "Where's Blue?"

He seemed taken aback, disappointed. He was still hoping for the devil reincarnate—and what was I? A white knight? His face slackened. I'd ripped his heart out without even touching him.

"Who is this Blue? Are you not the agent of your evil government? Are you not some zealous thug sent by your superiors to kill the ultimate villain? To kill *me*?"

"I'm Cloud, and I came here for Blue. Where is she?"

Several grenades exploded. The whole compound was on fire. Evidently the rough riders were very keen on a scorched earth policy of justice. Daleen hurled me away and I landed on my back. He raised his hands to the heavens and asked the unseen, "What do you want of me? I am *your* Prophet. I am the Arch Angel and you have sent me a worm to defeat in my greatest moment of tribute to you."

His plea with God, or whoever, gave me the time I needed to recover. I struggled to my feet and saw this was a *man*, and I didn't want to merely kill him. I wanted to break the spirit of the beast. I wanted him to die questioning his God.

"Where's Blue?" I yelled.

He ignored me, bellowing open-armed toward the sky, "I am so much more worthy than that sniveling long-haired son of yours. I am the man of action, the warrior. I deserve the ultimate adversary and you have sent me his piss boy."

Pulling the Randall knife from its sheath, I channeled into his spirit of immortality. I felt the freedom of not believing you could be hurt or die. I flashed the blade in his direction and repeated the question, which seem to cause him so much pain. "Where…is… Blue?"

A ten-ton ball of fire slammed into my left arm. Shocked, I looked down to see a seething gush of blood soaking my shirt. I blinked and saw a man standing not ten yards away holding an AK-47 rifle. The man was yelling an affirmation towards Daleen. He leveled the rifle into a holding pattern with my head, and just at that moment the griffon that was Earl stepped close and gutted him. Earl looked in my direction, the knife dripping warm blood. I gave him a smile of heart-felt thanks, and he disappeared back into the chaos.

"Daleen, I asked you a question, now going on four times. Where is Blue?"

He climbed down from Olympus or that mountain where the Ark crashed. He looked at me like the bug he thought I was. Light dawned on yonder forehead. "You're here for the deputy, aren't you? You have no further purpose other than rescuing the maiden. You are her suitor?"

I wanted to cut Daleen. I wanted to cut him a thousand times and let each bleeding wound be held to a white-hot flame. But I was hurting him more by being the worm. "Where…is…Blue?"

"I will remind you imp, she is of no consequence. She is the gravel my road to the right hand of the Father is built upon. Of course, I fucked her, cut her, and beat her. She was grist for my immortal mill."

I wasn't exactly sure what he was saying, but I knew he was soiling Blue. I gathered all of my mental reserves against the worst of answers. "Did you kill her?"

Before he could reply, a voice rang out. "No! I'm here."

It was Blue, bloodied and battered. She had the evil, hungry grin of a wolf when it knew the kill was at hand.

Before Daleen could react, she jumped forward, and with all of her weight buried a huge shard of aeronautical glass into his right eye. He shucked her off and let loose a howling scream that cut through the deafening explosions of gunfire and grenades. Daleen staggered around, pulling at the glass buried in his face. Blue bounced to her feet, ripped the shard from his hand and cut so deeply into his throat I thought his head would fall from his body.

She stood over the half decapitated corpse huffing with satisfaction. She was both the most terrible form I'd ever witnessed and the most beautiful woman I'd ever seen.

**

I hobbled over to where Blue stood. She dropped the long saber of bloodied glass and I enveloped her in my arms, blessing whatever powers that had let me find her and embrace her one more time. Her arms were pinned to her side, and after a full minute of the bear embrace she began to squirm. I didn't lessen my grip, tilting my head back so I could look into her eyes. The *look* was there, the eternal flame.

She smiled and said, "You're breaking my back."

I held her at arm's length so I could examine her. She was badly beaten. Her clothes were ripped and torn. Her fingers dripped blood from the cut of the glass. On her face was a long, curving wound. Through her makeshift halter-top, a dark, burned swatch of skin showed. I went to move the shredded shirt away. She pushed my hand aside. This was my Blue, beautiful even through her own gore.

Movement nearby caught my eye, and we pushed away from each other ready for the next battle. I had almost forgotten the carnage going on around us, feeling the rapture of holding Blue again. The rain was a full-out downpour. Lightning and thunder writhed to slice and rupture the woods. Rufus Ford staggered from beneath a hanging oak branch. Propping him up was the indelible form of Mildred Hayes.

The old man wore the one and only true smile I'd ever seen on his face.

The front of his denim work shirt was sliced open in parallel lines, as if a grizzly had taken a swipe at him. Blood edged each of the torn shreds.

He said, "Well I reckon these old boys' bull-killing days are just about over. There was a hell of lot of them, but there are only three still pulling air as far as I can see. Earl and Bean have 'em tied up over next to that half-moon building. I think they're more ashamed they didn't die with their comrades than having killed so many bulls and people. I was just coming over to see what your take on things is. I think we should just go ahead and kill 'em, make this thing a damned shut out. I would've already done it, but that big bruiser Earl wouldn't let me. He said they quit at some point, and he wasn't going to let anybody kill people who were so obviously broken."

Mildred interrupted. "Did ya get my money before ya killed the sorry bastards?"

For the first time in many days, I felt a smile of my own. I looked at Blue. Her mind had already processed the carnage and was ready to take official control again. She walked over to Rufus and planted a big wet, bloody kiss on the old man's gray sandpaper cheek.

"I'll never be able to return this favor. You are an amazing man, and I'm proud to know you."

I can't say for sure, but I believe I saw a brief sparkle in the gruff man's eye. He raised a brown calloused hand and brushed the hair back from Blue's face and said, "Ditto." Then he turned to me. "I reckon I'll take this old woman, and me and the boys are going to head out of here before the law shows up in packs. I guess you folks didn't really see what went on here, did ya?" His intent was clear. Rufus Ford wanted to go back to his quiet ranch and try to forget the nightmare. I nodded. Ford turned and limped away under the arm of Mildred Hayes, back to the big semi tractor-trailer where the rough riders were calmly and orderly loading the huge horses.

The fires were still burning high. As we both looked toward the big truck, a shadow fell over us, and before I could wheel around, King Kong Bean grabbed Blue in his massive grip and held her up toward the sky. He was beaming, more proud than any successful expectant father. Earl walked up and put his hand on Bean's shoulder and gave him a look that said, *calm down.* "Bean, the lady is bleeding. She's hurt. Don't you go and make it worse."

I walked over to the three of them, and, encircling them, I brought us together into a group hug, a huddle. We raised our heads and looked at each other's bloodied, worn bodies. I opened my mouth to tell the boys how much I owed them for this, but Earl cut me off. "Don't. Don't say a damn word. If you act like we was doing you some kind of favor, I'll beat your sorry ass myself. We're family, and family don't need no thanking."

I said instead, "You boys better go ahead and high tail it out of here. Mac is on his way with what I imagine is a whole pack of FBI agents. It would probably be better if you weren't here."

Earl nodded and Bean put his big mitt over my face and I saw a tear leak from his eye through his wide-spread fingers.

Chapter 56

And then, we were there, Blue and I. Standing amidst fifty-something dead bodies and three huddled, scared-out-of-their wits camouflaged men. I interlaced her fingers with mine and we walked hand in hand to the center of the smoldering compound. Within five minutes, every deputy sheriffs' car, CDLE vehicle, and many more plain cars I didn't recognize skidded into view. MacGregor Knox, in his custom-made Chevy Silverado, was first to arrive. He roared into the compound with lights flashing and sirens wailing.

Before the vehicle could even come to a complete stop, the passenger door flew open and Emma exploded in our direction. Looking ten years older, she grabbed us both in one huge embrace. For only the second time, I saw Blue cry. The moment their bodies touched, both of them began to shake violently with deep sobs. I left before the rain of tears became contagious. I walked over to Knox, who was looking at us, satisfied yet heart-felt worry on his face. He doubled over at the waist, resting his hands on his knees in the stance of a winded runner.

I stood beside him for a very long few minutes. When he recovered and stood upright, he looked at me with a false indifference. "I reckon you probably can't tell me just what went on here can you?"

The well-placed circular statement made me smile. I looked at him and said, "No. I reckon I can't."

A very official-looking, strapping young man approached Knox. He was wearing a dark suit and wrap-around black sunglasses. Knox nodded in my direction, "This is Cloud, my ummm, my friend."

I looked wide-eyed at him, then caught myself. The agent offered his hand and spoke with very clear enunciation. "The disease we were worried about wasn't Bovine Spongiform Encephalopathy or Mad Cow disease. The CDC did some tests and it actually turned out to be Crappie, a nearly harmless cousin to Mad Cow that isn't contagious to humans at all. I'm not sure what all went on here, but we'll need to get some statements and formulate exactly what we'll say to the press. I'm sure they'll be here any minute."

I reached out and patted the FBI agent on the arm and said, "You can tell them *the* devil went down to Cable and only took the souls that needed to go."

EPILOGUE

A month later, on a Sunday, our normal day of doing our own thing, I looked from the front porch out onto the garden. The main theme was abundance. No matter which direction you looked, there was green, and flowers, and green, and flowers.

It was roughly six o'clock in the evening. Both of the ladies were decked out in their gardening clothes with large floppy straw hats. They were covered in dirt and had a warehouse worth of gardening tools surrounding them. An overwhelming sense of warmth engulfed me, and I raised a Cuban cigar to my lips. I sat down in a rocker so worn it shrieked with my weight.

The press coverage had been immense. Every major network and cable channel sent reporters to the lowly Cable Counties. The story of Bent Daleen, the Prophet of Cable County, was already gracing the cover of Time Magazine with the caption, "Do We Really Know Our Neighbors?"

I thought to myself, *No, we really don't and I'm not sure I care to really know any of them.* I played a card game in college that asked questions. The intent of the game was to initiate intense, serious conversation. The one question I remember was, "Would you rather live for one week just as you do now with all of your family and friends, or would you rather live alone, completely alone, for the rest of eternity?" I smiled to myself. The answer finally seemed obvious.

The day before, I'd collected my fee. Tom Goodrich stood in his own front yard. He hemmed and hawed and whined. He even tried a couple of insults. But he wrote the check. He paid.

Later, when I handed the same endorsed check to Ben McCullers, he demurred. I'd already prepared my response. "That's absolute bull…"

***

Tito Salazar drove the truck through the historic streets of Barcelona, Spain. He took an English born, round-about at the coast edge of the ancient city and finally to an obscure back street. He backed into the parking lot and through the door of a large anonymous building.

A man from the Institute came out from the shadows and approached the truck. Tito fingered the bright silver bracelet on his wrist as he rested his elbows on the rail of the truck's bed.

"Did you bring our brother home?"

"Yes, he's in the box. He did not complete his mission, but only because the disease we gave him to deliver unto the herds of America failed. The American scientists through the American press, say it had something to do with the humidity and mosquitoes in that god-forsaken Florida. The heat and mosquitoes actually saved them. Otherwise he would have succeeded, even though at heart he was a fool." Tito Salazar handed the keys to the man from The Institute.

The man said, "Yes, well… The Institute's purpose is to incite fear—to terrorize and cause conflict. The American wide-bodies will still pause before each bite of hamburger for years to come. They don't trust their food supply. The mission was a success."

Ten minutes later, Salazar walked along the pedestrian highway of Barcelona known as Rambles. He headed in the direction of the Picasso museum. Perhaps an afternoon musing the Genius would put things back into perspective.

On his way a little girl stopped in front of him. He knelt down to say hello and she offered him a single red balloon. He took it, smiling, and continued on.

The End

Before You Go…

Become a Cable Native!

If you liked **ABSOLUTE BULL**, you'll love **BUG TROUBLE**, book #3 of the Cable Counties Thriller series, coming November 2016.

Visit HartleyStevens.com to become a **Cable Native** and receive the latest updates, short stories, and special offers.

About the Author

Hartley attended the University of Florida, studying exercise science, and he played football for the Florida Gators. A stint in the United States Army as a specialist in Criminal Law, followed with postings in Oklahoma, Indiana, Georgia, Texas, and South Korea.

His education continued as a world traveler. He and a friend set out on a one-year odyssey covering North America, New Zealand, Australia, the Pacific Islands, Southeast Asia, and both Eastern and Western Europe.

He lives in North Central Florida with his wife Jeanie, his son Brendan, and Maximum-Ready-Set-Go, an energetic pug/yorkie. His older son, Justin, is a United States Marine, stationed as an infantryman with 1/6 Hard, Camp Lejeune, North Carolina.

Acknowledgements

First and foremost, I thank, Alisa Jeanine Stevens, Jeanie, my wife. President of the 'Good Woman Club.' An every-day good attitude and the flexibility to learn and grow with me are the most treasured concepts in my life.

Andy Sherrard; every little boy wants to grow up and work with their best friend every day. I get to do it!

Thank you to my friend and teacher, Jani Sherrard. I hover over every sentence with your eyes and ears in mind.

Special thanks to the *Mind-Benders,* Kenny, George, & Andy. The accountability, creativity, inspiration, and honest conversation pushed me beyond trying and into doing—again.

Kate, for the creativity and building of a launch package that will not be rivaled.

My super-human launch party team, my Cable Counties family: Rob Orlando, Jody Phillips, Jamil Ahmad, Heather Todd, Jennifer Kolacia, Kristi & Todd McCray, Pattie New, Stacy Shine, Joli Day, Jen Blalock, Emmy & Matt Vincent, Lieba Gouin, Robbie & Rachel Stroh, Jill Parent, Leonard Blakeley, Mike Booth, Mike Booth Jr., Wickie & Julia Ariet.

Graeme Hague and Jessica Holland for a spectacular edit. Thank you for seeing what I could not. Marina & Jason Anderson with the Polgarus Studio for guidance and an exceptional format.

Sharon Julian for a world-crusher, platform building website.

Douglas Haines for original Cable music.

I honor the great teachers in my life: Big Danny, Daddy, every line can be traced back to something I learned on the farm; Catherine, I never thought anyone could tame the beast; Beth Hubbard, Mama, my first friend and the one who taught me unconditional love; Johnny, your reach and grasp always inspire me; Rex Stevens, my brother, the toughest human, period! Bethy Proctor, my sister, bike rides, junior cheerleader outfits, and the joy of hushpuppies. Jan Matkozich, my mentor, you bought me books, taught me how to really read and helped me learn how to laugh at myself because you enjoyed laughing at me so much. Joe Cirulli, my boss, you gave me an education, trusted me, and gave me a stage on which to practice. Bill and Bobbie Dye, my in-laws, thanks for showing the rest of us how a man and woman should live and love their family.

Tonya and Jennifer, my wonderful sisters-in-law who support their sister when she feels like a writer/business widow.

Craig Standridge and Craig Wainwright, my brothers-in-law, for technical support and firearm knowledge.

I would like to thank my two sons, Justin and Brendan. I wouldn't ask for the lessons, but I'm glad I'm learning them.